"I wouldn't recommend running away."

Nasir sat to block the tent's opening, his rifle laid across his knees. "It's safer here. Nobody will hurt you now."

"Why?" Sadie asked cautiously.

"Because you're mine." The words fell from Nasir's lips slowly, distinctly. "I claimed you in front of the others."

"No." She squared her body toward him, prepared to fight. If she could disable him, maybe she could stay hidden in his tent until nightfall, then take off.

"It'll buy you time to find a safe way out. I'm here for some information. As soon as I have it, I'll take you to the nearest village."

Was he lying so he could catch her off guard later? She watched him and weighed his words. He hadn't hurt her, not once. "Are you an undercover policeman or something?"

"Hardly. But you *are* safe in my tent."

DANA MARTON

UNDERCOVER SHEIK

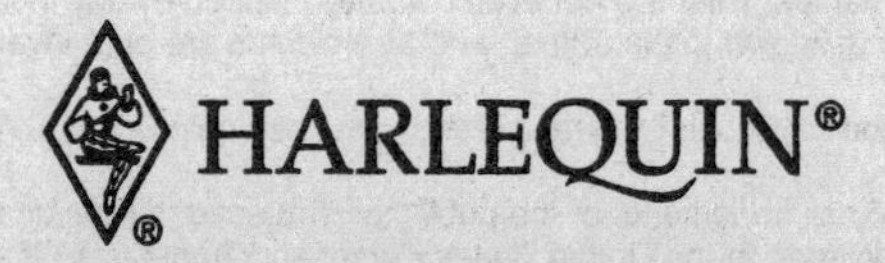

TORONTO • NEW YORK • LONDON
AMSTERDAM • PARIS • SYDNEY • HAMBURG
STOCKHOLM • ATHENS • TOKYO • MILAN • MADRID
PRAGUE • WARSAW • BUDAPEST • AUCKLAND

With many thanks to Allison Lyons and Maggie Scillia.

ISBN-13: 978-0-373-88736-1
ISBN-10: 0-373-88736-1

UNDERCOVER SHEIK

This edition published by arrangement with Harlequin Books S.A.

www.eHarlequin.com

Printed in U.S.A.

ABOUT THE AUTHOR

Dana Marton lives near Wilmington, Delaware. She has been an avid reader since childhood and has a master's degree in writing popular fiction. When not writing, she can be found either in her garden or her home library. For more information on the author and her other novels, please visit her Web site at www.danamarton.com.

She would love to hear from her readers via e-mail: DanaMarton@yahoo.com.

Books by Dana Marton

HARLEQUIN INTRIGUE

806—SHADOW SOLDIER
821—SECRET SOLDIER
859—THE SHEIK'S SAFETY
875—CAMOUFLAGE HEART
902—ROGUE SOLDIER
917—PROTECTIVE MEASURES
933—BRIDAL OP
962—UNDERCOVER SHEIK

CAST OF CHARACTERS

Nasir ibn Ahmad—The brother of the king of Beharrain, Sheik Nasir is determined to keep Majid from starting a civil war and killing his family to regain the throne. But when he goes undercover among bandits, he finds more than clues to Majid's whereabouts.

Sadie Kauffman, M.D.—Sadie was kidnapped by bandits from a field hospital in Yemen. Can she trust the most dangerous among them, Nasir, to save her life?

Majid—He swears to regain the king's throne and kill anyone who stands in his way.

Umman—He is the leader of a group of conscienceless bandits and one of Majid's supporters.

Saeed ibn Ahmad—Beharrain's rightful king and Nasir's brother.

Dara Alexander—The American woman who made headlines around the world by marrying Beharrain's king.

Ali—He works for the royal stables. Is he involved in something sinister or is he just at the wrong place at the wrong time?

Abbas—A clerk at the royal palace. He owes much to the king, but maybe he's motivated more by greed than gratitude.

Chapter One

Dr. Sadie Kauffman had been always skeptical of people who, as their death sentence neared, claimed to have changed and reformed. Now she believed it. Time made all the difference, being locked up with nothing to do but think. She'd had forty long days and nights to mull over what her life had been so far—a mad race for things that in hindsight didn't matter. She *would* live differently. She rubbed her fingertips together. They tingled from nerves. Today was the day of her execution.

She watched one of the bandits as he plodded toward her makeshift prison, his rifle slung across his shoulder, his face wrapped in the trailing end of his headdress to protect him from the blowing sand. He opened the low door that had been nailed together from pieces of scrap wood, and swore at her as she stumbled out awkwardly, her legs numb from her cramped quarters.

"Move it," the man said, and although she was limping forward as fast as she could, it wasn't quick enough for him. He shoved his rifle barrel between her ribs to make her go faster.

She blinked toward the desert horizon. The sun had barely breached it. Her last sunrise. No, she wouldn't think like that. She had to have hope. If the desert bandits killed her, what would they gain? They had to keep her alive to collect the ransom. She'd spent the night working out different ways to convince Umman, the camp's leader, to extend the deadline.

It'll work. They need the money.

She ran her fingers over her black headscarf and attached veil to make sure they exposed nothing but her eyes. The man kept shoving her at every few steps, toward the tents instead of the cooking fires as he would have on any other day.

"It's as fast as I can go," she snapped

without heat. Did he even understand her? Other than Umman, the rest spoke no more English than the few words they used to order her around.

Her sandals sunk into the hot sand with each step. She still hadn't learned to balance her weight just right, angle her feet so she could walk the terrain with ease like the men whose tents sprawled like giant, unworldly beasts on the sand ahead. Most had their flaps open—giant, yawning mouths getting ready to swallow their prey whole. She shivered despite the heat that had to be nearing a hundred degrees already.

She halted at the entrance of the largest tent, looked inside with quick, darting glances and kept her head down to make sure her gaze wouldn't directly meet anyone else's. Most of the bandits were in there, lounging on worn carpets and sipping spiced coffee.

"So your country cares not if you live or die." The contemptuous voice was Umman's.

As far as desert bandits went, they looked the part—Ali Baba and all that—missing teeth, savage faces, murderous weapons. They smelled the part, too.

"The money is coming," she said with false confidence, knowing the U.S. never paid ransoms. She'd always thought that a reasonable policy—until now. "Today. It's a lot of money." Five million dollars.

The men didn't appear to be impressed with her promise, nor did any of them look like they might be sympathetic to her cause. She was nothing to them, less than nothing—an annoyance, a reminder of a business plan that didn't work out.

"You think me a fool." The leader's voice was low, yet it seemed to thunder across the tent. He was the oldest of the men, his face crackled with scars, his scraggly beard blending into gray as it fell to his worn brown robe.

She had no doubt he would cut her throat without thought, as he would cut a goat. As he had cut one of his own men not two weeks before for some minor insubordination.

"Your people show me great disrespect," he said.

Her carefully crafted speech had sounded reasonable and convincing in her head in the quiet of the night, but now, faced with a tentful of bandits, the arguments she had prepared suddenly seemed laughably feeble.

"I'm a doctor. You might need me. A few more days—"

"Do not bargain with me." Umman's voice rose, thick with anger. "We do not need your kind of medicine. You think I would trust you?"

Apparently not. At first, when she had been kidnapped from the hospital, she'd been convinced they'd taken her to heal some bandit chief and would let her go once she was done. It had taken her days to realize the true severity of her situation.

There had to be words she could say to convince him to do just that. *Think. Think!*

Something shifted in the darkest corner—a man she hadn't noticed, sitting away from the rest. She swallowed as she recognized the man she feared the most. *Nasir.* The sight of him scattered her few gathering thoughts.

Something in the man—an indefinable hardness, a dark purpose to his heart and murder in his eyes—made her get out of his way every time she'd found his gaze on her.

He was new to camp, had prodded in on his small camel two days after she'd been kidnapped from the field hospital. He had quickly gained the respect of the other men. There had been a fight or two at the beginning, testing the newcomer. Since then, most knew enough to steer clear of him.

His full attention was on her now, his dark gaze burning her.

Umman set down his cup and spoke in Arabic to the guard who'd brought her in while he dug through a wooden crate and tossed the man a new-looking digital camera.

He wanted her execution documented—probably so the next time they asked for ransom, everyone would know they were serious.

Her heart beat against her chest so hard it hurt. *This can't be happening. It isn't real.*

Things like this happened to other people, strangers on the evening news. Her hands trembled at the thought of her lifeless body on some Web site.

Run! her brain said, but before she could react, she was grabbed, rough fingers digging into her arm.

"Another day. The money will be here," she begged, her lungs drowning in panic that seemed to swallow her whole.

"Out."

The guard obeyed, pulling her from the tent into the merciless light, into the killing heat. He dragged her behind the tents, up the first dune, barely slowing as she struggled against him.

How much did she have left? Ten minutes? Five?

He held her tight, his gun aimed at her as he yanked her along. If she could pull away, how long would it be before a bullet slammed into her back? Even running couldn't save her now. Nothing could. Her body went slack with resignation.

She'd chosen the wrong course of action, staying in her prison in hope of a rescue instead of trying to run away in the night. The realization made her light-headed, dizzy. She'd thought the ransom would come, that the bandits wouldn't be so eager to discard their ticket to the money. She had no supplies. She'd been afraid the desert would kill her if she ran, but now even that seemed a preferable choice—death on her own terms.

"Let me go. Please." Her voice was high-pitched, weak. She hated it. Now that she realized there was no way out, she wanted to at least die with dignity.

If he understood her, he showed now sign of it.

She glanced at his gun. He'd use that. It would be quick; she wouldn't feel a thing. *Almost over now.* She didn't think they would go far. Umman just hadn't wanted the inconvenience of her blood on his carpets.

NASIR UNCLENCHED HIS FIST. In another five minutes the woman would be dead. Anything he could do to save her would jeopardize his hard-won cover, might make the other men realize that he was less than the ruthless killer he had purported himself to be.

And yet, he couldn't sit still and allow her to be gunned down in cold blood.

"I take her." He kept his voice hard, setting his face into an expression that bore no challenge.

A moment of silence passed, confusion underlining it. Most of the men were looking at him puzzled; Ahmed, the youngest, with burning hatred.

"I said she would die," Umman said, reacting just as Nasir had expected. The leader could not allow his authority to be overruled, especially not in front of his men.

No time to wait for a better opportunity, though, or to try to manipulate the situation.

"She'll be dead to her people. She'll be mine." Nasir stood, but inclined his head toward the man to make sure the action wasn't interpreted as a challenge.

Umman looked at him with blossoming anger and suspicion. He had every right. Nasir had been the one who had argued against allowing the men to rape her, and now here he was, claiming her as his own.

"She has no place here, no usefulness. If

you changed your mind and want to use her before she dies do so." The camp leader glanced around, indicating that went for everyone.

"I claim her for my own. She'll be taken by no other," he said fiercely, then added on a more subdued voice the first good excuse he could come up with, "She might carry my child."

A low murmur rose from among the men, some of amusement, some of outrage.

"She came to me." Nasir went on with the lie, unperturbed. If words could save her, he was willing to make up a tale. He did not want to start a fight, not yet. "Maybe she thought it would gain her favor. It does not. But I would have her birth the child. After my son is weaned, you may do with her as you please." He shrugged. "Once she's no longer useful, I'll kill her myself if you want."

Thick silence hung in the tent as one second passed, then another.

"Are you certain?" Umman asked, his face dark.

Nasir nodded.

Even among bandits, children were taken seriously. Most of the men had families in one of the many villages at the edge of the desert.

"If the child lives, if it's a boy, he would be my first son," Nasir added for emphasis.

Everybody understood the importance of that.

Tension thickened the air in the tent.

He listened for any sound from outside, willing the silence of the desert to remain unbroken, aware of every second that passed as he waited.

"She is your trouble." Umman gave his verdict after a few moments, visibly displeased.

Ahmed hissed. "She'll run away if he sets her up in a village. She knows where we are. Who we are."

The leader shot him a glance that shut him up and had him looking away, but did not berate the young man for his hotheaded outburst. He seemed to share Ahmed's concern.

"She stays with us," he said. "There's fire in that one that's not broken yet."

One of the men made a suggestion as to how Nasir could manage that, and others laughed, the tension suddenly broken.

"*Shukran.*" Thank you. Nasir nodded to the leader and gave proper respect, then hurried out of the tent to save the American doctor's life.

ANGER WAS SLOWLY replacing her fear.

Sadie tore her arm from the man's grasp, nearly toppling to the sand before she caught her balance and swirled back, hoping to catch him by surprise and ram him hard enough to make him drop the rifle. *Screw dignity.*

She was too freaked to pull it off anyhow, to stand there in the middle of the desert looking all noble and unperturbed, to think of some profound parting words her executioner wouldn't understand in any case. Following orders and being suitably submissive not to rouse anyone's anger hadn't gained her freedom. It was time she started to fight.

She wasn't doing well at it, she thought as the guard knocked her to the ground.

Keep coming up.

That was the key. She struggled to her feet and charged at him again.

He wasn't taking her too seriously, hadn't even bothered to call out to the others. He seemed undecided on whether to be annoyed or amused. She rammed her head into his stomach, hard enough so he staggered back.

Then his rifle barrel was pressed to her temple as he shouted at her in Arabic. Game over. Looked like he'd had enough entertainment.

Another shout came from behind her, then was repeated in English. "Stop."

She swallowed at the sight of Nasir striding over the sand, his long black robe billowing ominously behind him like a giant hawk descending on its prey. *Fearsome.* His face was unscarred, his nose straight, unbroken, unlike most of the rest of the men's. He was the tallest and toughest bandit in camp, but that wasn't what made him seem the most dangerous. He had something cold and hard within that showed in the set of his strong jaw, in his intense sable eyes. She found the overall effect chilling.

He yelled again, and she realized with

surprise that he was yelling at the guard and not at her. Had the camp leader changed his mind? Hope rushed to her head.

Then Nasir reached her, and his long fingers closed around her arm. Without another word to the guard, he dragged her off—not back to the main tent, nor to her makeshift shelter-slash-prison… She slowed and dug her heels into the sand when she realized their destination was his black tent.

"No," she said like she meant it, as if her knees weren't trembling under the worn *abayah* they made her wear. "No, please." She feared Nasir more than she feared execution. At least a shot in the head would have been quick.

Some of the men leaving Umman's tent stopped to watch as Nasir dragged her on effortlessly, paying no attention to her struggles. One shouted something in Arabic. Nasir didn't respond.

Then they were inside the tent he alone occupied—he did not share like the others—and he let her go so suddenly that she sprawled onto the carpets.

He stepped toward her, but she scrambled

away, looking frantically for a weapon. She dashed for the rifle that hung from the tent pole.

He got there first.

Her breath lodged in her throat. Fear raked its sharp talons down her skin.

"Take it easy," he said in near perfect English. "I'm not going to hurt you."

Her body went still as she stared. Other than a few grunted words, he'd never spoken her language before. A few seconds passed before she gathered enough courage to address him, moving slowly as far from him as the tent allowed.

"You'll wait for the money? How many days?" Even if all they gave her was a single extra day, she'd have tonight to escape.

"I wouldn't recommend running away," he said as if reading her thoughts, and sat to block the tent's opening, his rifle laid across his knees. "It's safer here. Nobody will hurt you now."

What part of her hostage-waiting-for-execution position did he consider safe? Surprised, she looked into his face, then quickly away when she realized her mistake. She'd been beaten by one of the other men for that in the beginning. She was to speak when spoken to and keep her eyes on her feet when not on her work.

But Nasir didn't become outraged. After a moment, she glanced back, hoping to read his true intentions in his expression.

"Why?" she asked cautiously.

He held her gaze for a while, his sable eyes burning into hers, his features hard with a large dose of displeasure. "Because you're mine." The words fell from his lips slowly, distinctly.

"Ah… What?"

"I claimed you in front of the others."

Mother of God, help me now. She could only imagine what he'd claimed her for.

"No." She squared on him, prepared to fight. If she could disable him, maybe she could stay hidden in his tent until nightfall then take off—provided that he didn't have any visitors in the meanwhile.

"It'll buy you time," he said mildly.

"For what?" Was he playing with her? Was it some sick game he wanted before he pounced?

"To find a safe way out. I'm here for some information. As soon as I have it, I'll take you to the nearest village."

Was he lying so later he could catch her off guard? She watched him cautiously and weighed his words. He hadn't hurt her, not once. Her fear of him stemmed from watching him with the other men. Emotions ran high in camp, and the bandits were often at each others' throats. Nasir hadn't started any fights, but he finished many.

"Are you—" She sat back down, trying to put the pieces together. "Are you an undercover policeman or something?"

"Hardly." He gave a rueful grin that softened his face.

She stared, a second or so passing before she said, "But you're definitely not going to hurt me?" She wanted to make sure that was nailed down.

"You are safe in my tent."

She would consider believing that if she was still alive and untouched by the end of the day. She eyed the curved dagger tucked into his sash. "So, who are you exactly?"

"Nasir."

She'd been hoping for something beyond that.

"A spy?" The question slipped out as it occurred to her. He had said he was here to gather some kind of information.

"I'm here on my own business."

And she would just bet his business wasn't the good kind. She hadn't been mistaken when she'd seen murder in his eyes. But as long as it didn't involve her and he would help her out of here, she was willing to overlook it.

"How long before you leave?"

"As soon as I have the information I came for." He stood, set down the rifle and pulled up an extra carpet, fastened it to the poles so it neatly divided the tent.

He moved like a warrior, unhurried, efficient. Who was he? Who had he been before joining the desert bandits' camp?

In some ways, he was very much like the others, just as tough and better in a fight, but a thin veil of civilization clung to him that set him apart, which was especially noticeable now that he let his guard down in front of her.

"Where did you learn English?" she asked.

He worked on fixing the partition without answering. "You may use this side," he said politely when he was done.

He was confusing the hell out of her. He would allow her out of his sight?

He surprised her further by handing her his dagger. "In case you need to defend yourself. Your continued stay does not make everyone happy."

She pulled the sharp blade from its sheath with hesitation and stared at it. Why arm her? She could kill him in his sleep.

"You could try," he said, guessing her thoughts again, and she could swear she saw a hint of a smile hover above his lips. "I wouldn't recommend it," he added before turning on his heels and ducking out of the tent.

She spent a couple of seconds staring after him before springing to action, realizing she was wasting a precious opportunity. For the first time in weeks, she was truly alone. Nasir's tent sheltered her from prying eyes as her prison never had with its wide gaps between the rough boards. She took a quick inventory. Two large water skins hanging from the main tent pole, several bags that looked like they'd been made of carpet remnants and a few bowls that were neatly lined up by the tent wall next to a stack of clothing.

She went to the water first and drank as much as she could without making her pilfering obvious. Then she rummaged through the bags and found food, small canvas sacks that held dried figs and some kind of jerky, probably goat. She hurriedly ate a couple of each as she conducted a thorough search of the tent. She found a cell phone and hope shook her hands as she tried to turn it on, but the battery was dead. It would have been too good to be true.

Still, for the first time since she'd been kidnapped, she had free access to food and water. *And* she had a weapon. Here, in front of her, was everything she needed to escape.

The more she thought about trusting Nasir's offer, the worse the idea of waiting for him to get her out of here seemed. She would be a fool to hang around to see if he would keep his word and take her to safety. He could change his mind. Umman could change his mind. Ahmed, who'd been after her from day one, could finally find an opportunity to do her real harm. She would never be safe as long as she was inside this miserable camp.

The only person she could trust was herself. She would save herself. As soon as night fell. Whatever she had to do.

I could kill if I had to. The thought came out of nowhere and took her by surprise. Yes, she could kill, although at a price to herself, both as a doctor and a human being. But she could. When backed into a corner, all living things fought for life.

She hadn't realized that, not until today when she was dragged from Umman's tent to be executed. Tonight she would do whatever it took to get away, even if it meant taking another life to save her own.

She tucked the dagger into the waistband of the pants she wore under her long robe. For the first time in her life, the presence of a weapon made her feel better. She stepped out of the tent with caution, intending to go no farther than the semisecluded spot behind the area where the dozen or so camels usually lounged, the place she'd been using to relieve herself.

She'd gone only a few yards from Nasir's tent, dodging the men who were going about their business, when Ahmed spotted her and strode over, his fat mouth set into a thin line of displeasure. He marched his pudgy body through the sand with jerky steps, keeping his small, dark eyes on her, yelling from afar. "Woman! Whore!"

She stopped, hoping he wanted nothing more than to give her some small, humiliating task as usual, like scraping goat dung from his sandals. She would quickly do whatever he required. Tonight she'd be free. She couldn't allow anything to get to her.

"You feed camels. Water camels," he said.

Taking care of the animals was his responsibility—every man had his own task to keep the camp running. He was probably angry that Nasir had stopped her execution. He was probably looking to reassert his authority over her, to show her that as long as she was in camp, she would remain their slave.

Sadie nodded, the very picture of obedience, and cast a worried glance toward the camels, making sure she looked fearful, hoping that would be sufficient. Ahmed usually left her alone once he figured he had tortured her enough for one day. If he thought the task left her trembling, he might be satisfied with that and not think up any further ways to distress her.

The animals were twice the size of camels she'd seen in Yemen at the market where the local Doctors Without Borders liaison had taken the group of international physicians she was a part of the day after their arrival at the small field hospital.

The trip to the market had been the first and last that she'd been able to participate in. Three days later, the hospital was raided, the supply room robbed. She had the misfortune of being inside it when the bandits had come.

"Work," Ahmed shouted at her and shoved her forward.

She moved obediently, semisecure in the knowledge that now that Nasir had claimed her, Ahmed could only demand work from her and nothing more. He had come to her during the night once before, insisting on another kind of service. By putting her body weight against the door of tightly tied branches, she'd been able to keep him out. Her prison, devised to prevent her from escaping during the night, had saved her.

He was yelling at her in Arabic, and she picked up the pace, walking toward the tent Ahmed shared with three others and the large bags of camel feed. She hadn't seen Nasir's shorter, leaner camel among the rest of the beasts. He'd probably ridden out of camp.

Her instincts prickled when instead of going off to enjoy having passed on his morning chores, Ahmed seemed intent on following her inside the tent.

"I feed the camels," she said as she stepped through the flap, keeping her head down in an attempt not to anger any of the other men she'd expected to find inside.

The tent was empty.

She couldn't step back. Ahmed was right behind her.

Get the work done, get out. Fast.

She went to the sacks, filled the bucket, moving purposefully, ignoring the bad feeling she was getting from the man who watched her.

He made his move as she was about to head back outside, blocking her way, looking at her with so much heat, so much hate.

"I'll feed the camels," she said and stepped forward to pass by him.

He wouldn't have it.

She was close enough now to smell his breath, the sour sweat of his body. Several weeks' worth of dirt was ground into his patched-up, faded camouflage uniform. She stole a glance at the look of determination in his face.

He was not going to let her go.

The dagger. Since she had the bucket in her right hand, she bent to set it down slowly, as if giving in to his will. But in a sudden move, he knocked the camel feed from her and had both of her hands pinned to her side. She struggled against him. He was strong, stronger than she'd thought.

"Stop." She fought back with everything

she had, kicking, trying to smack her forehead into his face, doing anything and everything to make up for not being able to use her hands. "Let me go!" Desperation gave strength to her voice.

The carpets tangled under their feet, making it harder for her to find her balance. She twisted and kicked backward, got him in the knee by pure chance. His hold loosened at last. *Almost clear.* Then she tripped on her robe just as he grabbed for her, and they went down together with a solid thud that stole the air from her lungs.

Chapter Two

"Civilian casualties will be significant."

Majid glared at the man who dared to voice his ridiculous concern. When a sculptor created a beautiful piece of art, was he criticized for the marble chippings he left on the floor? "If anyone dies, it's the usurper's fault. The people will understand that."

And once he was king again and the media was under his thumb, he would make sure everyone would see it his way. *Casualties.* Of course there'd be casualties. *Bismillah!* He was reshaping his country.

Those who committed treason *should* suffer. How quickly they had jumped to the usurper's side, forgetting their lawful king. They *should* be punished. The leaders of the traitors would be rounded up and taken care of—certainly his cousin's family. The others he would let live. He needed people if he wanted to collect taxes. He needed workers for the country he was even now preparing to birth.

"How many men do we have?" he asked his temporary council.

His secret advisors consisted of a few sheiks whose tribes were involved in weapons smuggling and as such benefited from his venture. Also those to whom he had promised land, and two semiinfluential industrialists who hoped for sizable oil contracts from his government once he was restored to the Beharrainian throne. All were enemies of the current false king, people he had angered by interfering with their business and limiting their income.

Today they all gathered to talk war in the large cave Majid was using as his headquarters at the moment.

"We have ten thousand men," the oldest of the sheiks said.

"That's enough." Saeed had less than that when he'd stolen the throne four years ago from Majid. He would pay for that. "Once that devil's spawn of a cousin of mine is dead and the palace is ours, the army will switch sides and follow their rightful king."

That's how it had been before—a lesson he had learned well. His entire army had deserted in a single day, seeing Saeed's rising power, fearing for their worthless hides. They were disloyal to Majid before. They would be disloyal now to Saeed.

"The time is here, my friends," he said as a calm settled over him. To rule was his destiny. "We will cut off the head of the snake and stomp out his nest."

Saeed, the false king, would soon be executed and so would his whore, his American wife.

He would spare only Salah, Saeed's son, eight years old now and fancied to be heir. For him, he had other plans.

His three-year-old twin daughters couldn't be allowed to live, either—they might have sons when grown. Nobody who could ever claim any connection to the throne and come back to haunt him would be left alive. That included Nasir, the king's brother. He was the more dangerous of the two. Had he taken any wives yet? Had he sired any children? He would have to be looked at carefully.

Majid took a sip of spiced coffee, then set the cup onto the stone ledge by his side. The first time he took the throne, he'd been lenient with his cousins. He would not make that mistake twice. This time when he was finished, they and everyone they held dear would be dead.

WHERE WAS SHE?

Nasir scanned the small camp. Her prison cell was empty. So was his tent. Of all the other tents, only one had its flap down. He strode toward that, fairly certain that he would find her inside.

She couldn't have run away, not yet. The desert was void of life around them as far as the eye could see. She couldn't have passed out of sight in the short time since he'd last seen her. And somebody would have noticed her walking away if she'd tried. Not that he didn't think she would attempt to escape. But she wasn't stupid. She would wait for a better opportunity.

The first sounds of struggle reached him when he was a few meters from the tent. He broke into a run, threw the flap open when he reached it and saw the desperate struggle on the floor.

"Ahmed!" Rage flooded him as he lifted the hefty bastard off the woman, threw him aside and stepped between the two, willing the man to fight.

"You had no right to her." Ahmed spat the words and charged, his face red with effort and fury.

Nasir was ready for him, his body braced. Ahmed had the advantage of weight, but the disadvantage of inexperience. Nasir ducked his blow.

Ahmed would be trouble over and over again until dealt with. Over the past weeks, he had developed a deep-seated hatred for Nasir. The man was way too hotheaded. Nasir relaxed his limbs and focused on the fight. He could not allow anyone to put his mission in jeopardy. He watched his opponent, noticing the way he shifted his weight and planned his next attack to come in low.

The only way to stop him for good was to kill him, but Ahmed was a distant relative of Umman, and Nasir couldn't afford to turn the camp leader against him until he got what he had come for.

"Son of a whore." Ahmed charged again.

Nasir turned, twisted so the man missed with the second punch and stumbled outside through the flap, pushed by his own momentum. Nasir stepped after him, waited for the next attack and dropped the bastard, nice and clean—with admirable restraint—in front of plenty of witnesses.

Without checking whether Ahmed was getting up or not—he wouldn't be…not for a while—Nasir stepped into the tent, grabbed Sadie by the arm and dragged her outside, making a show of it.

He couldn't find a single look of disapproval among the men who were gathering around. Good. They understood his actions and accepted it.

"Come." He pulled Sadie behind him roughly. They would expect that, for him to assume her guilt in the matter without questioning. Punishing her now for being in a tent alone with another man was his responsibility, his right, even if he deemed the necessary punishment to be death.

He shoved her inside his tent with great show but a gentle hand, then closed the flap behind them. Plenty of light filtered through the thinly woven side panels to see, the tent having been made to allow for the circulation of air.

"How bad did he hurt you?"

Her eyes brimmed with mistrust and fear. She pulled away from him a little too abruptly and backed into one of the tent poles, causing her headscarf and attached veil that had loosened in her fight with Ahmed to slip down now, coming to rest around her neck.

He was stunned by her short blond hair, barely covering her ears.

He didn't like it.

It seemed indecent—long hair was Allah's adornment for women. Still, for all that, the exotic color and shape suited her face.

She scrambled to cover herself, her eyes cast down, her fingers trembling.

"Leave it," he said. She belonged to him now, his tent was her home—an odd and uncomfortable thought. But it meant that even according to the strictest customs she was allowed to go unveiled as long as it was just the two of them.

She hesitated in midmotion, the fear and mistrust on her fair face undiminished.

It annoyed him. *Bismillah,* he'd never given her a reason to fear him. "I had to act firmly." He realized that he'd begun to pace, and stopped. "Umman's men would expect you to be punished."

Beharrain was on the path of progress, but in the outlying areas many people lived according to the strict rules demanded by Wahhabism. Majid's supporters, in particular, claimed themselves to be staunch conservatives, although their backward ideas had little to do with old customs or the words of the Prophet. Because of them, one could still hear news of women killed for tarnishing the honor of their families. They considered rape a woman's fault.

The American doctor lowered her arms and her head with them. And for some reason that defied logic, her supplication annoyed him.

"They expected me to be mad," he said, wondering if she could truly understand. And he *was* mad, although not at her. He would have gladly strangled Ahmed. "Are you hurt?" he asked again.

She nodded and said after a brief pause, "Minor bruises. Thank you for getting me out." But still, she wouldn't look at him.

From a woman of his own culture that would have been a sign of respect. From her, that she was still afraid of him felt like an affront.

What did it matter? Whether she feared or despised him had no significance. He could and would see her to safety all the same. They had no business beyond that.

"The dagger?" he asked.

She fumbled with her robe and produced it after a few moments. "Couldn't get to it."

He could see why and cursed himself for not thinking of it before. The task was cumbersome. She had to gather up the folds of her long *abayah* first. He fixed the problem by stepping up to her and grabbing the black material, ripping a four-inch hole in the side where her hand could fit through if she needed to access the dagger in a hurry.

"That should do." He hadn't anticipated Ahmed to go this far this fast. At least the humiliation of his public loss should keep him in check for a few days. Nasir stepped back and prayed to Allah he wouldn't need any more time than that.

In another day or so, the convoy they were all waiting for would be coming. He would do whatever it took to get Majid's whereabouts from them. There was a connection between Umman and Majid, he was sure of it.

"Stay clear of Ahmed. As much as you can, stay in this tent." He could not look away from the golden hair that curled at her nape and around her ears. He'd seen western women before—he'd been abroad on occasion and didn't much care for it—but she was in his tent. "If you must step outside—" She would have to, if nothing else than to relieve herself. "Cover up."

"How long before we go?" she asked, everything about her hesitant.

But he'd had a few glimpses of another woman, one that he suspected was the true Dr. Kauffman. She'd been different when he'd first arrived to camp. And when she'd fought her executioner this morning, she'd fought like a tigress.

"A few days," he answered her question.

Her gaze was cast at her feet, thick, dark-blond lashes shading her eyes. Perhaps so he wouldn't see in them that she had no intention of staying that long. He said nothing, knowing it would be pointless to warn her.

She would do what she thought was necessary.

Then he would do whatever needed to be done.

NASIR LAY IN THE DARK and stared at the ceiling of the tent. It had to be past midnight.

The American woman, Sadie, had been gone for about two hours.

He didn't blame her—he would have done the same—but neither could he let her go to her death. What did she know about the open desert?

He would wait another hour or two before he went after her—enough time for her to realize the mistake she'd made. She was on foot. She would be exhausted by then and lost. She would know she had failed. He had to wait that out—he couldn't afford to watch her every second of the day. For her own sake, she had to accept that staying with him was her best chance for survival.

In general, he believed that the fewer foreigners in the country, the better. Most of them came to his part of the world for gain, at the expense of his people. He trusted only one, Dara, his brother's wife, another American. Dara would want him to look after Sadie, but it wasn't his only reason for doing so. He was Bedu and he lived by the code of the Bedu, the *sharaf,* part of which was protecting women.

There were some religious fanatics who considered only Arab women worthy of protection, not even the women, really, but their virtue. And if they deemed that lost, they thought it just and right that the woman should be killed, that they were worthless without it. Anger boiled in his blood at the thought. Never had the Prophet, blessed be his name, required the killing of the innocent.

He was conservative and proud of it. There was much in his culture he wished to preserve. But he had nothing to do with this new breed of religious devotees who sought to rule by terror, preach purity in the streets, then engage in the vilest acts of immorality behind their walls. And these fanatics who'd had free reign under the previous king were now plotting against the new ruler, Saeed, Nasir's brother.

Nasir looked up to the ceiling of the tent and swore to Allah he would stop them. As long as there ran blood in his veins, he would protect his people and his family. And beyond them, he would protect all who needed his help. He was Bedu.

SADIE WALKED FORWARD in the sand, pulled her headscarf from her pocket and mopped her forehead that beaded with sweat from the effort. She'd decided to leave it off until the sun came up and grew hot enough to necessitate cover.

Her small pack of food and water seemed to weigh thirty pounds. She adjusted the sack over her back. She was thirsty, but was determined to ration what little water she had. She was tired, but resolved not to stop until sunup, to use every minute of cool air for walking. She moved forward toward a bright star she could not name. By keeping to it, she made sure she would go in a straight line instead of in circles.

Other than that one precaution, she was pretty much lost.

When she'd started out, she'd walked in the direction Nasir had rode in from a few weeks back. He had to have come from somewhere.

She hoped it wasn't another bandit camp.

God, he confused her.

He was some grade *A* badass, to use an expression she'd learned from a ten-year-old boy she'd once treated for a broken leg in the ER. And yet, Nasir had saved her from execution, and then saved her from Ahmed. Why? For himself? He had claimed her. God, did he know what century this was?

He would see her to safety, he'd said. She

wasn't about to trust anyone who had anything to do with the people who'd kept her captive.

She glanced behind her as she had from time to time, although if the bandits came after her, she figured she would hear the motors of their pickups before she saw them. The moon provided enough light to walk by, but she could see only a fraction as far as during the day.

She yanked her right foot as it sank into the sand. The foot came up, her sandal didn't. She leaned her weight on the other foot to search for it. The fine sand seemed to be crumbling around her, flowing like water. She tried to brace herself, waiting to touch solid bottom, thinking it a windblown spot where the soil was looser. She was in up to her knees before she realized the seriousness of her situation.

Quicksand.

"Help!" The terror-filled cry tore from her lips without thought, dousing her with desperation once it was out. Who could help her here? Nobody. There was none.

She tossed her bag clear, tried to tug her

feet free, no longer caring about the sandals. But as soon as she made headway with one foot, the other sank deeper. She squirmed. *No.* She had to stop that.

Spread the bodyweight. She remembered some childhood advice on what to do if the ice cracked on the pond she and the neighbor kids had used for skating in the winter. The same principle should apply here. She lowered herself onto the top of the sand, hoping she could somehow crawl to safety.

But within minutes, she was in to her waist and knew there could be no way out.

Stop. Stop. She forced herself to stay still instead of madly scrambling like instinct pushed her. She held her breath, watched the sand. She was still sinking, but slower now.

How long did she have? She had sunk up to her chest in about fifteen minutes. If she hadn't moved at all, could she gain another fifteen? What would be the use? What were the chances that someone happened along? Yet the instinct to survive would not let her give up. She grappled desperately for an idea as she held her body in iron control, utterly still, to buy herself as much time as possible.

Fifteen minutes.

She wouldn't think of what would come after that. She was a doctor; she knew what it meant to die by suffocation.

She tipped her head to look at the stars.

The sand squeezed her, held her tight. She kept her arms above it, her neck stretched once she sank to her chin. A few more minutes. She took deep breaths to keep the panic at bay. Then the sand came over her mouth. The desert sand had the consistency of fine dust, unlike the gritty beach sand she'd known all her life, and it felt like drowning in talcum powder.

When the sand covered her nose, panic kicked in and she could hold still no longer. She thrashed, made it to the surface for another full breath, called out again, her subconscious mind flashing a name, "Nasir!" before she went completely under. She couldn't stop struggling now even knowing each movement took her under faster.

Her lungs burned, stars growing and exploding behind her closed eyelids.

She clamped her mouth shut against the reflex to open and try to gulp nonexistent air.

As her hands, the last of her, went under, she clawed at the sand. She thought she heard a shout. Hard to tell over the blood that rushed loudly in her ears. Maybe the voice had been nothing but a trick of her oxygen-deprived brain. Then something solid brushed against the tip of her fingers, and she jerked to get back to it. She desperately searched around, clinging to the last few seconds of life she had.

A hand wrapped around her wrist and heaved hard. She started to come up little by little, her lungs ready to explode. She was barely aware now what was happening, focused with the last vestiges of consciousness on the strength of the hand that was pulling her back from death.

WHEN HE'D BEEN A CHILD, he'd had nightmares about quicksand—torturous dreams that had seemed to go on forever. He used to wake in terror, covered in sweat, gasping for air in the night.

Reality was worse, Nasir thought, and hung on to the slim hand, holding his breath under the sand. He jerked his right foot—he had dove in headfirst and his right foot was the only part still above ground—and yanked on the rope again, urging his camel to a faster walk. Ronu obeyed and pulled he and Sadie up, inch by slow inch.

Soon his head was free, and he took his first breath of air, coughed out the sand that had gotten into his mouth.

"Faster!" he yelled at the camel in Arabic and yanked the rope again.

The arm he held under the sand had gone limp.

He pulled with all his strength and once the hand was up, he let it go and reached below, hooked under her armpits. As soon as her head appeared, blue-faced and barely recognizable, he stopped and reached into her mouth with his fingers to clean out the sand.

He put his ear to her lips.

Nothing.

Ronu kept pulling. He paid little attention to the animal now, barely registering as they reached solid ground again after a few seconds. He called out to the camel to stop, then turned all his attention to the woman in his arms. He wiped his hand then reached deep into her throat with his fingers to clear it, flipped her over his arm, thumped her back to dislodge anything else that might be in there. When he turned her once more, he sealed his lips to hers and forced air into her lungs. He was probably blowing some sand into her air pipe, but he had to take that chance. If he succeeded in reviving her, she could cough that out.

He pulled away and pressed his ear to her chest. A second passed then another. He breathed for her again then swore as he waited for signs of life.

You should have come after her sooner.

He would have, but he had run into Ahmed, who'd been lurking around her old shack, and they'd had words. He had to make sure Ahmed was settled before he could ride off into the desert.

He pressed his lips to hers one more time,

ignoring the sand between them, and pushed air into her.

And then she coughed, *al hamdu lillah!* Praise God.

"Sadie?" He called her name, shook out his *kaffiyeh* and used it to wipe her eyes, then pulled the flask off his belt and poured some water on her face. Drop after sandy drop rolled off her eyelashes, her cheeks, her lips.

Her eyelids fluttered and she raised a sand-covered hand on reflex to rub them. He held her down and used more water instead to keep her from rubbing in sand.

She was coughing in earnest now, a terrible, choking sound, but a sound of life nevertheless that filled him with relief.

He helped her sit. "Sadie?"

She drew wheezing gulps of air and looked dazed and lost. "What happened?" She could barely get the words out, but her face was turning a healthier color.

"You walked into quicksand."

Her expression changed as she remembered. Her hand clamped on to his arm and wouldn't let go.

He'd seen Dara like that with his brother, Saeed, when something was wrong with one of the children. Bedu women comforted each other. Western women seemed to require this also from men.

He considered putting his arm around her, but it didn't seem honorable to touch a woman like that who was neither his sister nor his wife.

She solved his dilemma by having another coughing fit and collapsing against him.

His back stiffened in surprise, but he found himself reluctant to pull away. He tapped her slim back a couple of times, gently, awkwardly, giving thanks to Allah when her coughing quieted.

She didn't have much of a body under the long, ample dress. He hadn't realized that, her fragility. She had stood up to every hardship she'd encountered since he'd met her, endured whatever Umman and his men had thrown her way.

She pulled away after a few seconds—too soon. She wasn't nearly steady. He hadn't minded offering her comfort. The contact seemed to calm him, too. Having her that close, touching, was a good reminder that she hadn't been lost. He had gotten to her in time.

He would never forget the sight as he rode over the last dune and saw her head break free from under the sand ahead, her last breath used to call his name.

He cleared his throat. "Rest. We have time."

She rubbed the sand off her hands then did her best to clean it out of her neck, her hair.

"In a few days," he said to reassure her, "I will see you safe. You can't walk through the desert alone."

"I think I figured that one out." She coughed briefly, looking at him fully in the face again, for the first time since their short initial talk in his tent.

A long minute of silence passed, then another.

"Why did you save me?" she asked.

He looked back at the round indentation just a few feet away, the patch of ground that could have taken the both of them.

"My father was swallowed by quicksand," he surprised himself by saying instead of trying to find an answer to her question.

She seemed to pale, although it could have been a trick of the moonlight. "I'm sorry. That's— It must have been terrible."

He untied the rope from his ankle at last, ignoring the burn on his skin, and stood. He unhooked the other end from Ronu's saddle and rolled the rope up, put it away. He brought back more water for her, picked up his rifle from the sand and swung it over his shoulder, then stuck his handgun into his sash while she drank. He sat cross-legged in front of her, at a respectable distance.

"Can you not tell me who you are?" she asked between gulps.

"I'm not a bandit," he said, and hoped she would believe him this time.

"THEN WHAT ARE YOU DOING with them?" Sadie shot back. "How do I know you're not going to sell me for my kidney to some rich oilman on dialysis?"

She wasn't entirely joking. She had

treated just such a patient at the field hospital the day before she'd been taken by the bandits. The young man, not yet eighteen, had been kidnapped from the streets of his village, taken to a private clinic where one of his kidneys had been removed for an illegal transplant. He was treated until recovery, then dropped back off at the same spot, his pockets stuffed with money.

Not that this kind of thing happened every day, but the point was, it did happen. Then there was the sex slave industry and other lovely possibilities she didn't care to find out about up-close and personal.

"I'm Sheik Nasir ibn Ahmad ibn Salim ben Zayed."

"Sheik? As in king?" Whatever she'd speculated about him over the past weeks, she wouldn't have guessed *that.*

"No, no. Sheik of my tribe," he said modestly.

His olive skin seemed darker in the moonlight, his black eyelashes speckled with sand. How far under had he gone into the quicksand to get her?

"My brother is the king," he added.

She gaped. "King of what?"

"Beharrain."

That explained a few things. Nasir's excellent English for example. Beharrain's queen was an American woman. Dara somebody. She would be Nasir's sister-in-law.

"Are we in Beharrain?" The possibility occurred to her suddenly. Had the bandits crossed the border with her to the small kingdom to the north?

"As a Beharrainian, I would say yes. If you ask a Yemeni, they would say we're in Yemen. If you ask a Saudi, they'd tell you we are most certainly in their country."

Oh. They were in the desert where Beharrain, Saudi Arabia and Yemen met, a vast area where borders were sometimes fluid, sometimes nonexistent. To indicate this, they were drawn tentatively with dotted lines on the map.

"We're in no man's land—no army, no police—a haven for bandits, smugglers and the odd terrorist training camp," he confirmed her thoughts.

She pressed her knuckles against her

eyelids for a long moment. In hindsight, she might have been a tad optimistic thinking that she was just going to walk out of the place. She shook her head and muttered, "I suppose I've been embarrassingly naive."

"Courage is never worthy of embarrassment."

"How about foolishness?" She looked at him.

"You're safest with me." He held her gaze.

And she wondered if it might not be best to try to believe him. "So what are you doing with the bandits?"

"I'm looking for someone. It's personal." His face hardened into his fierce warrior look.

"And when you find him, you'll kill him?" she asked, then added in a more subdued voice, "I'd prefer the truth, even if it makes me uncomfortable."

"Yes." He said the single word without looking away.

"You can't leave him to the law?"

"The law had him. He escaped from prison."

"What did he do to you?"

He took a slow breath. "He killed my father."

Confused, she tilted her head. "I thought you said he was swallowed by quicksand."

"He was shot. His horse, with him still in the saddle, was forced into quicksand to cover it up. Then my enemy stole the country and murdered my people," he went on.

Was he talking about the previous king? She remembered something vaguely from the media. "Wasn't he made to stand trial?"

"Once my brother took power, yes. But he escaped from prison and now he is gathering followers, planning on assassinating the rest of my family and taking back the throne."

"So your brother sent you after him?"

His lips stretched into what might or might not have been a reluctant smile. "Saeed has infinite faith in the laws he restored, in the system, in his army. He still does not fully realize how far Majid will go to regain power. My brother thinks I'm on vacation in Paris."

"Paris?" She blinked.

With his headdress and tattered black robe, a rifle slung over his back and a handgun tucked into the sash at his waist, he didn't look like the typical sightseer around the Eiffel Tower.

He caught her glance skipping over him and tipped his head, the expression on his face, the look in his sable eyes hardening. "All Arabs are not thieves and murderers. We are like any other people. Sometimes, we even go on vacation."

"I didn't mean to imply—" Had she offended him? She forgot whatever she was going to say and came up with another question. "Why are you looking for the old king here?"

He watched her for a moment before answering. "Majid is using the area to recruit. I followed his trail. He has some connection to Umman. A smuggler's convoy is coming in any day now. They will bring guns Majid is sending. I'm going to talk to the men on the convoy and find out where he is now. Then I'll go to him. I will take you to safety on my way."

"Thank you," she said and shook the last of the sand from her hair, then realized her headdress wasn't anywhere around.

The quicksand had swallowed it. A shiver ran down her spine as she glanced at the spot. "And thank you for coming after me, for saving my life again." When she turned back to Nasir, she found him watching her.

"We should go," he said.

She stood at once and went for her pack a few yards away while he called to his camel. Ronu, she remembered his name. He was sleek and beautiful, different from the camels Umman kept that were twice as tall and several times as bulky.

She petted the animal's neck before Nasir talked him into lowering himself to the ground. She got on without trouble. She'd never had any fear of animals. In her experience, men were far more dangerous.

"Well done," Nasir said when he was up behind her and Ronu was standing. He sounded surprised.

"I used to ride horses," she explained.

"He usually spits at strangers who come near him."

"Is he bad tempered?" She leaned forward so she could pet the animal's neck again. "He seems nice to me."

Nasir's response was a single grunt as he nudged the camel to walking. After a few minutes, once she got used to the swaying caused by Ronu's uneven gait, she settled into her spot and enjoyed the ride.

"He looks different from the others," she said.

"A different breed. Umman's camels have been bred for smuggling."

"That's why they look like tanks?"

"They can carry extreme loads over long distances."

"What was this one bred for?"

"Racing."

She could picture Nasir flying across the desert like some angel of vengeance, his dark robe billowing behind him. The sight would be fit for a movie screen. "How fast can he go?" She half turned in the saddle.

He looked at her with a dangerous glint in his sable eyes. "Would you like to see?"

She nodded, trusting him to know what he was doing.

He'd saved her from execution, from rape and from quicksand. Knowing who he was—the Beharrainian king's brother and not a bandit—set her at ease. And that he spoke her language helped, too.

She was alive. The thought hit her out of nowhere and a sense of giddiness came with it. How many times had she faced death in the last twenty-four hours? She didn't want to think of it. She was alive!

As Ronu gathered speed, she bobbed perilously, until she stopped fighting it and let her body slide against Nasir's. His solid bulk behind her had a steadying effect. Many Arab men she'd seen so far had a slight build. Nasir didn't. He was strong and tall, wide-shouldered. And he was on her side.

She *was* going to make it out of here. A few days, he had said. That was all his business would take. This time next week she would be home.

Chapter Three

"It's amazing," she shouted over the pounding of hooves.

He had thought she would be scared once they got up to full speed, but she seemed thrilled. By the ride, or simply happy to be alive. He had never ridden with a woman before and with a man only when he was a child. Camel saddles didn't accommodate two people well. She was practically sitting on his lap. Nasir kept his eyes on the horizon.

"Do you ride horses?" she shouted back the question.

"Sometimes."

His tribe bred some of the finest horses in the country. But there was a thrill in a good old-fashioned camel race that those who participated in found addictive.

The animals could take on long-distance races that lasted several days across the desert, arid terrains no horse could have handled. Not every contestant made it to the finish line, nor every animal. These races tried a man. There was something primal, uncivilized about them, and often made him imagine his grandfather racing madly on a raid.

And that image brought to mind the bandit camp and Umman, even though they were a far cry from the honest raiders of the past.

"Your people did not pay your ransom," he said. "Why?"

"Policy. If one kidnapper got money, everybody would start hunting for Americans."

He could see the truth in that. If someone close to him got kidnapped he wouldn't pay, either. He would hunt down the kidnappers and kill them, take back what was his. "Your people are looking for you?"

"I'm sure they are, but Umman moved the camp after they took me. I kept hoping somebody would find me…"

"I found you," he said. "You'll be fine." He would see to it.

Her body was covered in her black *abayah*, her head wrapped in his plain white *kaffiyeh* against the rising sun. When she half turned, he caught a glimpse of golden hair escaping at her temple. "Why are you helping me?" she asked.

He owed as much to his sister-in-law. Sadie was from the same country as Dara. "You are a woman in need, alone. In our culture, every man owes his protection to such a woman." Both of those reasons were true, and yet even together they didn't explain the protective urge he felt for her.

"Could have fooled me," she muttered.

"Umman and his men are criminals." He did not want her to think ill of the country and culture he was so proud of. He could explain, he supposed, about the honor of the Bedu, but he wasn't sure she would care. "You do not have enough sick people in your own country?" he asked. "Why did you come to Yemen?"

"Seemed like a good idea at the time."

"Dangerous."

"Yes." She nodded. "I underestimated that. I thought I knew the risks and that the probability that anything would happen was slim enough to be acceptable."

"And your family?"

"No time for one. I don't need a man to be happy," she said.

Happiness was beside the point. "You need one to be safe," he explained.

"Not in my country."

That might have been the case, but she certainly needed one in this part of the world. He wasn't married, but he had sisters. He knew what kind of responsibility that brought to a man. Sadie had no one in this country. "I will protect you while you are here."

He should be able to do that—see her safe at a friend's house while he hunted Majid. Then when he was done, he would come for her and take her back to the palace with him where she would be truly safe until her return to her own country. Dara would be happy to receive her, he was sure.

She stayed quiet for a long time before she said, "Thank you."

He took a deep breath, satisfied in the

knowledge that he was doing the right thing. For the next few weeks, Sadie Kauffman would be like a sister to him.

He fixed that thought in his brain and ignored the way her lithe body felt as she rode in the circle of his arms.

SADIE WATCHED THE CAMP and forced herself to stay on the camel that was taking her closer. Now that the tents were near, her euphoria of having been saved from sure death was wearing off quickly. Coming back went against all her instincts. She'd escaped. For a few hours, she'd been free.

And she would be dead by now if not for Nasir, she reminded herself. She had to trust him.

"We've got visitors," he said and slowed Ronu to a walk.

A few seconds passed before she, too, spotted the beat-up Jeep that she hadn't seen before. Once they were close enough, she could even make out the license plate—Yemeni.

She scanned the camp for strangers, but couldn't spot any among the men who were out and about. One of them yelled over to Nasir.

She felt him stiffen in the saddle behind her. "What did he say?"

"The convoy is arriving today. A messenger rode ahead."

The sudden hardness in his voice made her turn to him. He was looking toward Umman's tent, the fierce intensity back on his face, darkness shadowing his eyes, tension tightening his mouth.

For a man who'd waited over a month for this very opportunity to gain information he needed, he didn't look happy. Sadie, on the other hand, felt full of hope all of a sudden. As soon as he had his information, they could get the hell out of here. "You think we'll be able to leave soon?"

"As soon as I can get my cousin's whereabouts out of them." Nasir made the camel lie down and slid off his back then helped her to the sand.

She stood aside, giving him room to unsaddle the animal. "How big do you think the convoy is?"

"I don't expect more than a dozen men."

She didn't look forward to having more scary-looking, battle-hardened bandits and smugglers in camp. "Will they stay long?"

"A few days, probably. Long enough to rest for the return journey. It would be best if you stayed in my tent as much as possible while they are here."

"No problem." She wasn't going to argue with that.

"Stay behind me," he said, his voice laced with annoyance all of a sudden.

She soon saw the reason. Ahmed was strutting toward Nasir's tent, derision on his face as he waited for them.

He said something in a hissing, hateful tone.

Nasir responded coolly and passed by him as if he weren't even there.

"What was that about?" she asked once they were inside and Ahmed had strode off.

"Envy." Nasir shrugged. "Because I have you and he can't."

She watched him in the dim light—his dark shape that dominated the tent, his noble features—and for a moment she wondered what it would be like to truly belong to a man like him. And then it occurred to her that there might be some woman somewhere who did belong to him.

"Do you have a family? Wife and children? Wives?" She corrected herself when she realized he might have more than one. The thought boggled her mind.

"I'm alone," he said, and something in his voice made her think the statement went beyond his marital status.

"You have your sisters and your brother," she said. At one point during the ride back, she'd asked him about the royal family.

"I have taken the path of revenge." He tucked the saddle in the corner of the tent. "My brother will not understand it. He's grown up with your western ideals, went to school in England. Forgiveness and reconciliation are his best friends, leaving the law to deal with the lawless." He didn't sound bitter as much as resigned.

"It works in a lot of countries, you know."

"It will never work with a man like Majid." His voice heated up. "He and I are more like our Bedu ancestors. He won't stop until either my brother or he is dead."

"So you'll fight him?"

"My life belongs to my king and my people," he said simply. "I'll go see what's going on."

She looked after him as he slipped through the flap. He had a strong sense of loyalty and honor that seemed almost archaic when compared to the type of people she was normally surrounded with. Not that there weren't any ethical people at the hospital in Chicago, but lately it seemed more and more doctors were concerned only with their fees and their next promotion. The backstabbing had been constant. Less and less attention was paid to the patients, treatments dictated by the insurance companies. Somewhere under the gloss of the color brochure picture the hospital paid millions in PR expenses to produce, there was a sense of futility and betrayal.

She had lived it, but she'd been too busy trying to get ahead to stop and think about it, let alone *do* something. In the last couple of weeks, she'd finally had the time and she *had* thought. She had realized that coming to Yemen had been a mistake. Not because she'd ended up being kidnapped, but because she had come for all the wrong reasons. She'd come because she thought it would look good on her résumé. She thought it might give her advantage over the other candidates and help her become department head when she returned home.

Only when she was forced to slow down and faced death did she realize how little her title mattered. What about her life? What about the life she was supposed to live—the one that held joy, the one where she would travel for fun instead of to conferences, the one in which she would make a difference instead of becoming part of a heartless, ineffective bureaucracy? She had thought she was making excellent choices along the way. She had gotten ahead. But in hindsight, she wasn't making choices at all; she was living up to expectations not her own.

She'd been good in biology and chemistry. Her biology teacher in high school had been a med school dropout so she steered Sadie in that direction, perhaps to make up for her own past. Her mother had been ecstatic when she'd announced her choice of career—something to brag to her girlfriends about at the Italian-American club. She did well in school and landed an excellent residency because that was what smart would-be doctors did. After her residency, she was offered several jobs and picked the best, just as anyone else in her place would have done.

But with success came expectations and fulfilling them took all her energy and every second of her day. Her career was a train, moving ahead on a set of tracks that led to a supposedly enviable future—except that the ride had stopped being fun a long time ago.

The wisdom to finally see this was given her by the desert, and she would be forever grateful for that. She was thirty-five and had almost died without living a single day of the life she'd meant to live. The thought scared her. She wanted to make it out of here so she could start over.

She went behind the divider and took off her clothes, shook the sand from them then put them back on. When she was done, she walked to the flap and peeked out in time to see Nasir coming toward her and a pickup rolling out of camp.

"Where are they going?" she asked, standing aside as he came in.

"Riding out to greet our visitors. Where is the dagger I gave you?"

She fished it out and handed it over, wishing he would let her keep it. Of course, he needed it more. For the most part, she planned on hiding out in the protection of his tent.

He pulled a thin strip of cloth from his pocket then reached for her left hand without warning, his long fingers looped loosely around her wrist. "I've been thinking about this," he said as he pushed up her sleeve. He wrapped the sheathed dagger to her left forearm upside down then rolled her sleeve back over it.

"Like this." He took her right hand, folded her fingers around the hilt and in a rapid movement pulled the sharp blade with ease. "Always go for the heart."

NASIR SAT in Umman's tent with the rest of the men, but his mind was not on the conversation. He hoped he could gain enough information from the arriving convoy to lead him directly to Majid.

He raised his head at the sound of trucks rolling over the sand. Since the tent had its long-side open in anticipation of the visitors, he could see them from where he was sitting—three old, canvas-top military trucks.

When the trucks stopped in the middle of camp, men jumped from the cabs and from under the brownish-yellow canvases. He counted fourteen of them.

One immediately began giving orders. The short hairs at Nasir's nape bristled as he stared at the man's profile. Was it— The man was slimmer than he remembered, but Nasir supposed it wasn't unusual to lose weight in prison. Then he turned and there was no longer a doubt.

Majid.

What was he doing here?

Nasir tamped down the anger that nearly brought him to his feet. He was in the worst possible position to draw his cousin's attention. He wanted to face the bastard, but not yet, not when he was surrounded by two dozen of his murderous supporters.

He needed to get the man alone, but if he was spotted first, he might not get the chance.

Would Majid recognize him?

In the tent, there was no place to go, nowhere to hide. And if he left now, he would have to walk right by the bastard. Nasir wasn't wearing the colors of his tribe, but he had not changed much in the past three years since the trial where he had testified against his cousin. Yes, Majid would know him.

He pulled back, as far away from the fire as possible, to keep to the shadows for as long as he could. He tallied the men, measured distances.

Could he take Majid here? Maybe. If his cousin sat close enough and didn't look around too carefully right at the beginning. Nasir judged the distance he could reach by leaping across the small fire.

Or he could use his gun, although that wouldn't be nearly as satisfying. Either way, he would be dead the next second, brought down by the rest of the bandits, but the thought that Majid would be dead before him was enough.

Except for Sadie.

He had no illusions of what would happen to her after he died. He glanced at Ahmed, who watched him with open contempt on his wide face.

Nasir's fingers crept closer to the handle of his pistol. Could he get off two shots? Would it make a difference? With Ahmed or without him, Sadie's prospects in camp without a protector were slim.

The visitors came in and fanned out around the fire, each giving their respect to Umman and greeting the rest of the men. Then Majid came.

"*Assalamu alaikum.*"

"*Walaikum assalam.*"

He exchanged greetings with Umman, then the rest. The voice, the face—older now but just as full of self-importance—heated Nasir's blood to the boiling point.

The man he had hunted for the last months, the man who had killed his father and was presently plotting to kill the rest of his family, was before him. He hung back in the shadows, although discovery seemed inevitable now.

And then the moment came. Majid's small brown eyes rounded in surprise.

"Nasir!" He came to his feet, his gun drawn.

Nasir stayed sitting, forcing a calm he did not feel, gaining satisfaction from the flash of fear in his cousin's eyes.

Not yet. Not yet. He held, no matter how difficult sitting still proved. Going after Majid now would condemn Sadie to death. He let the thought bind him.

"Cousin." He said the greeting in a voice that didn't show what it cost him to remain civilized.

"What's the meaning of this?" Majid was yelling at Umman now, his men standing behind him waving their own rifles. "You take for your friends my enemies?"

The insult had Umman coming to his feet, which had his men coming to arms fast. The two groups stood face-to-face for a moment, until Nasir began to hope they might fight. In the ensuing chaos he just might be able to reach Majid, then get Sadie away from camp before anyone figured out what happened.

But Umman reined in his men. "Explain yourself," he demanded from his visitor, his voice cold. No man would allow himself to be insulted in his own tent, not even by a dethroned king on the run.

"Sheik Nasir ibn Ahmad ibn Salim ben Zayed." Majid nodded toward Nasir. "King Saeed's brother."

That seemed to unite the two sides, as all of a sudden all guns pointed at him.

He knew no fear, only resolution.

"I spit at the king," Nasir said, and spat into the fire. He could help neither Saeed nor his country nor Sadie if he was dead. "It can be cold in the shadow of as great a king as he thinks himself to be," he said with derision. "He goes against everyone who doesn't obey his every whim. I left Beharrain to make my own fortune."

"Hand over your weapons," Majid ordered.

He shrugged and did so. "You have nothing to fear from me, cousin."

"If you broke with your bastard brother there would be news of it," Majid said, his eyes narrowed.

"He is too embarrassed to have managed to turn his only brother against him. He tells everyone I'm on vacation in Paris." He gave his cousin a meaningful look. "We both know he's clever with a lie."

The man seemed to be hesitating.

"Send someone to Beharrain. Someone who can get into the palace and get the palace gossip. They'll prove to you I'm telling the truth."

"I have such men." Majid kept his rifle aimed at him. "I have heard nothing."

The thought of having spies that close to his brother and his family filled Nasir with cold rage, but still he kept his calm. "Then your men's connections aren't as you think," he said, holding Majid's gaze. He could not back down, not a single centimeter.

Majid turned slowly from him to Umman. "I demand this man."

The camp leader hesitated, then nodded, probably feeling responsible for unknowingly harboring one of the enemy. And probably, too, Majid had promised him substantial rewards once he was restored to the throne.

"You may do with him as you wish."

"Hold him until the trucks are emptied, then tie him up in the back of one," Majid ordered his men. "We will question him further tonight."

He knew what that meant. Majid's torture chambers were infamous during his rule. But he let himself be restrained and led away. Fighting now would bring nothing but instant death. He needed a delay, even if it came with a price.

He swore to his ancestors that he would stay alive long enough to see the American doctor safe. Then, whatever cost it brought, he would settle his long-standing bill with his cousin.

SADIE WATCHED THE CAMP from the safety of Nasir's tent, hidden behind the closed flap. A few men were still moving about; the rest had settled in for the night.

What had they done to Nasir?

She'd seen him forced into the back of one of the trucks earlier in the day after the cargo of wooden crates had been unloaded. He hadn't appeared since.

Was he still alive?

Not knowing the answer hit her harder than she would have expected. He was alive, she told herself. Of course he was. Why would they keep him up there if they'd killed him? If they were to execute him, wouldn't they have taken him to the desert?

She listened, but couldn't hear anything from the truck that stood too far from where she was. Two guards had gone up with Nasir. They were still there. Food and water had been passed under the canvas at noon and at dinner time.

Nasir was under guard for some reason. What had happened in Umman's tent when the visitors arrived? What would they do to him now? Were the visitors going to take him away when they left tomorrow?

Fear shot through her at the possibility.

She was alive only because she'd been under Nasir's protection. She'd spent the day watching through the gaps in the tent, waiting for them to come for her. But Umman and the others must have forgotten about her in the chaos of receiving a large group of visitors. Nobody had as much as looked toward the tent that hid her.

And she'd been smart enough not to remind them of her existence. She'd stuck to the tent, drank no more than a few sips of water from one of Nasir's bottles, ate nothing but a single strip of camel jerky to make sure she didn't have to step outside to relieve herself until it was dark enough to do so without discovery.

Nobody had come for her so far, but sooner or later somebody would remember her. Ahmed, if no one else. She had to get away before that happened.

"Come on, go to bed," she whispered, willing the two men still out to retire for the night.

A good half an hour passed before they obliged her.

The heavens were more cooperative. Wisps of clouds drifted in to dim the moon, leaving the camp shrouded in darkness.

Four men were left on guard just outside

camp. Two more were in the back of the truck with Nasir. At least one of them would probably stay up to keep an eye on him through the night.

She selected a few dates and strips of jerky from the supplies she had gathered during the day, raiding Nasir's stores, stuck a flask of water under her arm, opened the flap and slid into the night.

The sentries sat at their posts with their backs to her, watching the desert. Still, she kept to the deep shadows where her long black dress made her virtually indistinguishable from her surroundings.

She'd made sure her new makeshift headdress—a dark blue strip of cloth she'd found among Nasir's belongings—covered her light hair and foreign face, leaving only her eyes free, which she kept downcast as she pulled aside the canvas on the back of the truck and pushed forward the food and water.

One of the guards asked something sharply, which woke the other.

Fear slashed through her. She bent her head even deeper, but didn't slink away.

Somewhere her new life was waiting. She wouldn't let anyone take that away from her.

The man came closer, swung his rifle over his back to reach for the plate. She handed it over then, quicker than she'd ever moved before, she clamped with both hands onto the guard's left ankle—about level with her chin as he stood in the back of the truck and she on the ground—and pulled with all her strength.

He fell to the sand with some clamor, dropping the plate and banging his rifle along the way. But the next second she had her dagger at his throat, and he took her seriously enough to keep quiet.

The other guard inside the truck asked something she figured for, "What happened?" or "Are you okay?" Then came the muted sounds of struggle, followed by silence.

A few seconds later, Nasir slid off the back of the truck.

"Go back to the tent," he whispered and took the dagger from her.

She obeyed without a sound. Nasir came in not five minutes later.

"I gathered food and water." She pointed at the saddlebags.

"Good."

She couldn't make his face out in the near complete darkness.

"You wait here." He gave her back the dagger then produced another blade from under a carpet, and a pistol, too, that he tucked into his sash. "I'll go see about the sentries." He slipped into the night without a sound.

She looked after him, but lost him to the shadows almost immediately. Her gaze settled on the truck that had held him all day. The canvas was down as before, no body on the sand, nothing to indicate the struggle that had taken place there just a short while ago.

She pulled back, checked the straps one more time to make sure everything was good and secured. Then she waited, praying for his safety.

He slid into the tent as quietly as he left it.

"Everything okay?" she asked.

Instead of answering, he grabbed her by

the shoulder and pushed her down roughly. Then he was on her, his weight squeezing the air out of her lungs.

The voice that whispered strange, hard words into her ear was not Nasir's.

Ahmed!

He remembered her at last. Or maybe he had remembered her all along, but had bidden his time until the whole camp fell asleep, not wanting to ask for Umman's permission, hoping to make sure he'd be the first of the men who got her.

She fought back silently, not daring to cry out as his hand pushed up her dress and his fingers dug into her thigh. She didn't dare to wake the camp.

She had to get to the dagger, but her left hand was pinned under the man's weight.

Her knee came up on reflex, but he avoided it.

No! She struggled, anger overtaking her initial surprise and fear. To hell with Ahmed. He was *not* going to win. She brought up her right elbow sharply to his temple.

That stunned him long enough so she could pull her left arm from under him.

He said something in a voice full of hate, and she could feel cold metal low on her belly.

He moved, but she was faster. She thrust her dagger into the man's heart with surgical precision, had enough presence of mind to leave it there to stem the flow of blood, at least until she was out from under him. She pushed against his bulk to get him off, not an easy task.

"Are you all right?" Nasir was there and tossed the body to the side.

"Fine."

"He's dead," he said, sounding surprised.

She stood, getting shaky now, taking deep breaths to fight the light-headed feeling that assailed her.

She had patients die now and then despite her best efforts, simply because their bodies were too damaged to live. This was the first time she had ever willfully taken a life instead of fighting tooth and nail to preserve it. Her stomach turned over. She couldn't look at the body.

"We need to leave." Nasir grabbed the camel saddle with one hand, the saddlebags with the other.

She nodded and followed him.

They moved with care, watching for anyone who might wake in the night, but the camp seemed to sleep soundly. She couldn't see a single sentry.

The camels woke when they came among them, but made little noise. Ronu gave Nasir no trouble when he saddled him, perhaps sensing the danger in his owner's mood.

He helped her up first and sat behind her, one protective arm on each side.

She held on as Ronu stood, unable to relax even when the animal settled into a slow walk, grabbing the saddle tighter when Nasir urged him into a trot once they were a safe distance from the tent.

"Where are we going?"

"To Mirem, the nearest Beharrainian village."

"How far?"

"Three days on Ronu," he said.

She hoped she could handle it. At least the food and water she'd packed should be enough. "Why did they turn against you?"

"My cousin, Majid, was with the convoy

and he recognized me." He told her what had happened in Umman's tent.

And she realized just how close they both had come to being killed. A chill ran through her. "You're lucky to be alive."

"He's lucky to be alive," Nasir said darkly.

That, too, she thought, grateful that Nasir hadn't tried to take his revenge on the man and damn the consequences.

Her eyelids felt heavy. She hadn't slept in a long time. She struggled to keep them open, then gave up after a while. Ronu was walking at a comfortable pace. They couldn't afford to wake the camp up by breaking into a gallop. The swaying saddle and Nasir's reassuring presence behind her had a soothing effect.

And yet, when her dreams came they were dark and filled with evil creatures that hid beneath the sand and tried to suck her down to them. One of them had Ahmed's face. The gruesome image startled her awake. She was surprised to find light dawning on the horizon.

She sat up straight, pulling from the safe

cocoon of Nasir's arms—her back had come to rest against his chest during the night.

"You slept enough?" he asked.

"Almost." She dismissed the nightmares and focused her awakening brain on what waited for them, a difficult couple of days, at best.

"I want to ride as far as we can before the air gets too hot, another hour or two. Then we'll stop to rest."

"I don't suppose there's an oasis near here?" She glanced back at him. His face looked drawn and bloodied. She hadn't seen that in the darkness of the night. How badly had they tortured him? "Are you all right?"

He shrugged. "My cousin thought my presence in camp was part of some large, elaborate trap set by my brother. He wanted details."

"Let me take a look at you." She could help. She should know the extent of his injuries.

"When we stop," he said. "We'll rest soon. The sun will be too hot to keep on moving. Then you can do with me as you wish."

She *wished* for a medical helicopter. For the first time, she noticed the odd way he was sitting, and wondered what kind of internal injuries he had sustained.

But she turned to face forward, accepting his decision, careful not to lean against his body again, not to put her weight on him. She would have given anything for her medical bag just now, anything at all for a bottle of disinfectant.

"When was the last time you had a tetanus shot?"

"In school. It's mandatory."

"How long ago?"

"At least twenty years."

Great. She kept silent for a while, then couldn't help herself. "Does it feel like anything is broken?"

"Maybe a rib or two," he said as if it were no big deal.

She could only imagine how uncomfortable it must have been for him to ride all night, to support her weight.

"What's that?" She listened, and a few seconds passed before she could identify the sound of trucks.

Nasir was scanning the horizon behind them and pointed. After some staring, she could see three dark dots that appeared to move.

"They are catching up with us," he said and urged Ronu into a run.

Chapter Four

They were coming into a rocky spread of the desert, one that seemed to go on and on for miles, with peaks that were as tall as ten feet in places, and a labyrinth of valleys between them.

"If we could get into the thick of that, we might be able to find cover," she called back over her shoulder as she leaned forward and hung on tight to the saddle pommel.

Ronu was dashing forward at full speed now, spurred by not only his master but the sound of guns behind them.

Guns!

She flattened herself to the camel's mangy fur. If she came any farther out of the saddle, she would fall.

"They can't hit us. They're too far," Nasir

shouted over the noise of the hoofs and braying and gunshots as he held on to her.

Then they made it behind the first row of taller rocks and behind that first row was a second, taller yet, then another and another, a maze of narrow canyons some ancient glacier must have dug millions of years ago.

They were going much slower now, the stony ground uneven and littered with boulders of various sizes. Nasir seemed to know just where to turn, at what spot to cross from one side to the other.

"Can we lose them in here?"

Her newfound hope evaporated as Nasir shook his head. "Not for long. The rocks only cover a couple of square kilometers. Eventually we'll have to come out into the open desert again."

He must have noticed her shoulders slumping, because he added, "We can hide for a while and rest."

She nodded. A temporary reprieve was better than none.

He maneuvered Ronu deftly, turning yet again, going up an incline this time. At least an hour passed by the time they made their way through the maze of rocks and reached sand again. Nasir stopped the camel and glanced around, his eyes narrowed to slits, scanning the line where the sand and rocks met, examining the ground toward the east first, then to the west.

"Are we looking for something?" she asked.

"El Amarra."

"Have you been here before?"

"A time or two." Before she could ask him to explain, he nudged the camel to get moving again. "There."

She couldn't see anything but more rocks. But as she looked harder, she saw that some were oddly positioned and one of the larger boulders showed patterns that resembled geometrical drawings rather than grooves carved by the elements.

The closer they got, the more of the carvings she could make out, flowing lines that bent into the shape of flowers and trees in a repeating motif.

"What is it?"

"An old trading city. The caravan route used to go through this way." He slid to the ground and helped her off. "I'm glad it's here," he said and moved forward. "After a bad sandstorm, places like this can disappear for decades, even centuries." He kept on going, looking at the stones closely as if navigating by them. "Here," he said finally and dropped to his knees to dig in the sand.

"What are we doing?" She went to help him without waiting for the answer. Whatever it was, it had to be connected to their survival.

"Looking for the well."

That made sense. They'd brought four plastic jugs of water; one was already empty. A shovel would have come in handy. The fine, loose sand seemed to flow back into place all too easily, making their progress excruciatingly slow. For every two inches they uncovered, one drifted back into place almost immediately. "How far down is it to the well cover?"

He nodded toward a broken pillar that protruded from the sand a short distance to his left. "Three or four feet. It's level with the foot of that column."

Three or four feet? That could take an

hour. "Do we have time for this? Can't we make it to the village on the water we've already got?"

He glanced up at her, his hands never stopping the efficient scooping movement she was trying to copy. "The well has been dry since before my grandfather's time," he said. "We'll use it to hide."

Her arm stopped in midmotion. Her muscles drew tight as she pictured the two of them huddled on the bottom of some ancient well, dozens of feet under the sand. What if the walls collapsed? She could still feel the weight of the quicksand pressing down on her, suffocating her. "I can't do it," she heard herself say, feeling dizzy.

Nasir looked up again and held her gaze. "Yes, you can. We must hurry. We don't have much time."

She couldn't. She really couldn't. Nausea washed over her, and she leaned forward. Sweat beaded on her forehead for a second before evaporating in the heat. Invisible hands squeezed her chest. She couldn't breathe.

She was having a heart attack.

She tried to think of what to do, but panic gripped her too tightly to think like a doctor.

Panic. Her mind grabbed on to the single thought. That's what was happening. A panic attack. *Breathe. Relax.* A few moments passed before her breathing calmed her a little.

"Are you ill?" Nasir stopped what he was doing and moved closer.

She pressed her hands to her chest, willed her madly beating heart to slow. "I'll be fine." She took another deep breath and let it out slowly.

"Here." Nasir was coming around and pulled her from the deepening hole in the sand, turned her the other way. "You hang on to this." He handed her the camel's rope. "And you watch for anyone coming."

His matter-of-fact voice and that she was no longer focused on the sand helped. She kept breathing deep and slow.

"Got it," he said triumphantly after half an hour or so.

She glanced back and watched as he cleared a round wooden lid about seven feet in diameter, lying well below the sandline,

He lifted it carefully and set it down, then came over to her and got a coil of rope and a box of matches from one of the saddlebags.

The gaping, dark hole brought the tightness back to her chest. "Maybe I could hide between the rocks?" Anything but to go down there under the sand. "I don't think I can go with you."

"We'll try. If it doesn't work out, we stay and fight." He bent to peer into the well. "Come."

She moved closer reluctantly, and could see a thick beam crossing the mouth of the well, walled into the rim on each end. Nasir was tying a rope around that.

"We'll go together," he said.

Deep breath in, deep breath out. She focused on her muscles and tried to relax them. She was having a psychological response to the fact that she'd almost drowned in quicksand not twenty-four hours ago. Her heart wasn't really going to stop. Her lungs weren't really going to collapse. All she had to do was to control her mind. Somewhere, she knew that descending the rope wouldn't kill her, nor would the well. There was air down there. Her symptoms were psychosomatic.

Knowing that and fixing the problem were different matters, however. Despite her best intentions, she balked.

"Now." Nasir came over to her and gave her a look of support and understanding. "We can't wait longer."

He took the camel's rope from her and led her by the arm to the mouth of the well. He went down first, enough so only his dark mop of hair was showing, his hands gripping the rope, his feet walking down the side.

He looked up and held her gaze. His face was calm, his body language full of strength and confidence. "Turn around and slide down backward." He let the rope go with one hand, reaching for her. "I won't let you fall."

She could hear the trucks again. They seemed closer than before. Hiding among the rocks would never work. She might not get captured immediately, but they'd find her before long. If she stayed, she'd be killed, she had no doubt about that. If she went with Nasir, she at least gave herself a chance. And him. He'd said he wouldn't leave her up here alone. He would stay and fight the men. She could only envision one outcome of that.

Okay. Let's do it then. She reached inside and found the courage and attitude she used when faced with a crisis at the hospital. Let's get it done...worry about how difficult it had been afterward at review.

Her *abayah* tripped her before she took the first step. The sound of engines was getting closer. She slipped the long dress over her head, balled it up and tossed it into the well behind Nasir. Then she turned and swung one shaky foot over the edge of the well, found foothold, went in with the other. With both hands on the rim, she lowered herself, kept bracing with her feet. And then her body met Nasir's and his hand steadied her.

"You hang on to me, I'll hang on to the rope. We'll be down before you know it," he said and let her go as soon as she got a good, firm hold on him.

Blood rushed so loudly in her ears, she could no longer hear the vehicles that hunted for them above. Her throat and chest constricted. She hung on for dear life as she tried to breathe.

A few moments passed before her surroundings came into focus again. She could feel the steady beating of Nasir's heart. He felt solid under her hands, and his strength seemed to calm her even as they dangled over the dark hole that looked ready to swallow them.

Save, she corrected. The well was going to *save* them. She had to believe that or she couldn't let Nasir take her down.

She tightened her hold on him as he began to move with the agility of a man who'd done this before. Maybe desert wells needed to be cleaned or checked or dug deeper from time to time. Wherever he'd gained his experience in handling the rope and negotiating the stone wall, she appreciated the fact that he had it.

The deeper they went, the darker it got. Their descent likely took fifteen minutes at most, but it seemed like two hours. He set her down, fumbled around. Solid ground under her feet brought some measure of relief, but she stayed close enough so her arm touched his. Then a circle of light appeared and dispelled the darkness.

They were standing on the sandy bottom of the well, five or six feet wide with dry, irregular walls.

His hand brushed against hers as he handed her a flashlight. "Try to save as much of the battery as you can. I have to go up to close the lid on the well and send away Ronu."

No! was her first thought. She could not stay down there alone. She grabbed after him, but touched only air.

He was already going up the rope. "I won't be long."

Panic rose inside her again, sucking the air out of her lungs, but she turned the flashlight off. They would need that battery more once the well lid was on and the darkness around them complete.

She looked toward the small circle of sunshine above that outlined Nasir's body as he progressed farther and farther away from her. What if he didn't come back? What if he got up there and it occurred to him that he could travel faster alone, if he decided to take his chances in the desert he knew like the back of his hand instead of being trapped with her in the bottom of a well?

She couldn't breathe again. *Stop. Stop. Don't think of that. Think of something, focus on something else, anything.* She closed her eyes and thought about what she would do when she got back to the U.S. She pictured her condo in minute detail, they way she'd toss her suitcases by the door and leave them unpacked until morning. She'd take a hot shower. Yes, that would feel good. She lifted her chin to let the imaginary stream wash down her body. She'd stay in that shower forever. She would order in. Chinese. And she would eat it sitting in front of the TV, her feet up, the air conditioner going full-blast. She'd have Tastykake for dessert. In fact, she'd pick up a whole bag of them on the way home from the airport.

A pretty picture; too bad she couldn't focus on it. Her muscles were cramped tight, her ears tuned to the noises that came from the surface. What was taking him so long?

Then wood scraped on stone above and inch by inch the shaft of light disappeared, shrouding her in complete darkness. She shivered, heard Nasir yell something unintelligible. To her? To the camel? She switched the flashlight on, in case that was what he wanted.

"I'm sorry, what?" she asked and looked up, breathing easier when she saw that he was on the same side of the well lid as she was.

No response came to her question, just a couple of muted grunts.

Breathe deep. He *was* coming back. *We won't be here forever.* She worked on relaxing her muscles, methodically, limb by limb. Then Nasir was finally there and she took her first full breath in a long while.

He dropped one of the saddlebags on the ground near her. "I brought some food and water."

She set the flashlight onto the sand and sat next to it. "Are you sure they won't find us here?"

He handed her a jug of water. "I smoothed over our tracks."

"And the well?" What if they opened it wanting water? The rope was still suspended from the crossbeam. What if one of them came down?

"I tied the other saddlebag behind Ronu so when I sent him off he would drag it, pushing sand over the lid."

"We're sealed in?" She swallowed. *Don't think of it.*

"We have plenty of air. Enough for the night."

"What will happen to Ronu?"

"He'll lead them on a good chase if they try to follow his tracks."

They fell silent for a while. She listened for the noise of trucks above, but when a sound came, it was a gentle whoosh.

"What was that?"

"The wind is picking up." He tilted his head and listened.

And she immediately remembered what he had said about sandstorms, how they sometimes buried these ancient ruins for years at a time.

"How bad?"

"Nothing to worry about. It's not the right season for a big one."

She hugged her knees and rested her forehead on them, holding tight while ready to jump out of her skin. Trusting anyone, putting her fate into the hands of another person did not come easy to her. Hers was a competitive field, everyone for his or her own. Women in medical school were a small minority. Women in leading medical positions were even rarer. She was used to fighting tooth and nail every step of the way, trusting only herself, taking charge and going after what she wanted. There were as much politics in hospitals as on Capitol Hill. She had gotten as far as she had by never allowing herself to depend on anyone.

And now she had to put her life into the hands of a complete stranger.

"So we'll sit here until morning?"

"They came after us in a hurry, probably without food and with little water. They can't stay long. They might leave a couple of men until the rest come back better prepared. We'll be gone by then."

He sounded confident and she allowed herself to believe his words because she needed to believe them to make it through the night.

"In the morning—" she started to say, but Nasir interrupted her with a motion of his head.

He stood and looked upward.

And then she could hear it, too, a faint noise, growing. Sandstorm, she thought at first but within seconds the noise was loud enough to make it out clearly—the sound of an engine overhead.

"I'm going to look around quickly then turn off the light. We need to save the battery."

"I want to clean your injuries." She reached for one of the water bottles.

"We can't afford to waste any of that."

"But—"

He dragged the back of his hand over his cheek. "It's not my blood," he said as he turned from her. He scanned the walls, the seam where the sand met stone on the bottom.

"Your ribs?"

"You can bind them in the morning. I won't be moving around much tonight." He made careful work of checking out the well.

"What are you looking for?" Her gaze followed the circle of light.

"Loose stones I need to watch on the way up, and stray scorpions."

She pulled her knees closer as her gaze darted around.

"Don't worry," he soothed her. "There's nothing."

His gaze held hers as the light went out.

She tried to keep the image of that in her mind, his dark eyes, the strong lines of his face, to keep from thinking of scorpions skittering forward from the cracks in the stone wall.

"Your parents must be worried about you," he said.

His voice seemed to dispel the dangers. "My mother," she said. "She didn't want me to come here." She'd never met her father, a German diplomat who'd seduced her mother at twenty then left the country when she'd told him she was pregnant.

"No father, no brothers?"

"None."

"No boyfriend?"

When she didn't respond, he said, "Or maybe he's here, searching the desert for you?"

"No. I had..." She wasn't sure what to call Brian. Boyfriend seemed too high schoolish. "We've broken up." And even if they hadn't, the idea of Brian coming after her to save her was laughably improbable. Brian would have asked whomever was handling her case for regular updates and went on with his schedule at the hospital as usual. It would have never occurred to him to try to come after her on his own. He was not the warrior Nasir was. In fact, no other man she had ever known before could quite compare to Nasir. She knew the strength of his body, could still feel his hard muscles against hers as he had lowered her into the well. In the tight space she was well aware of the intensity of his presence, even in the darkness. She was having trouble remembering much about Brian just now. Her senses seemed to be filled with Nasir.

"So what does a sheik do when not out to

destroy his enemies?" she asked, eager to distract herself.

He told her, his voice strong and comforting in the darkness. She clung to it as if to a lifeline. And maybe he sensed that, because when he was done he told her a story from his grandfather's time, then another and another, until she finally relaxed.

THE TRUCKS PASSED above them two more times during the night, but hadn't as much as paused. Their cover held. She slept little and fitfully, spent most of the night listening to Nasir's even breathing as his healing body took the rest it needed.

They made their way to the surface just before dawn, after she'd bound his ribs. Nasir first pushed open the lid to make sure all was safe, and then he pulled her up.

"What do we do next?" she asked, nervous now that they were out in the open.

"We wait for Ronu. He'll be back."

He'd said that before, but she only half believed him. The bandits could have gotten the camel or it could have simply walked off in search of the nearest oasis. If she could walk four days without water, that's what she would have done.

"Shouldn't we go back down until he comes back? What if somebody sees us?"

"I don't think they left more than a few men. They would be searching the middle, the narrow canyons where they couldn't go in with the trucks. They probably think we are hiding in the thick of things. They won't be looking at the edge of the desert. They circled around several times last night and didn't see us here." Nasir sat and leaned his back against the ruins.

After a moment, she did the same. His words made sense. She relaxed. "What is this place again?"

"El Amarra. The legends say it was a thriving city a couple of hundred years ago."

"What happened to it?"

"Once the railroad was built, the caravans stopped. Nobody came this way anymore. The people moved away."

She nodded and shivered a little in the cold of the night air. As hot as the desert was during the day, the surface of the sand cooled with amazing speed at night. Too bad they couldn't risk a fire.

She looked at the few standing arches, the delicate carvings. The sun was rising over the horizon, painting the sand pink and lighting up the ruins. The sudden unexpected magic of it took her breath away. "Wow."

Nasir glanced at her but didn't say anything. The silence of the moment was perfect, fitting the heartbreakingly vivid, sheer beauty of the place.

From the moment she had planned her trip with Doctors Without Borders, she had looked at it as a project with a deadline, a task that needed to get done so she could get her next promotion. There were several candidates for department head. She was the only woman, and the head of the hospital board was a known misogynist. She had to put something on her résumé that nobody else had.

Her trip to the Middle East was a means to an end. She hadn't expected to like anything, to make friends, to find beauty. But at that moment, as the sun rose and lit up the desert, the way the ruins seemed to sing touched her somewhere deep inside. She felt captivated. The tightness in her chest eased.

She stared at the ruins of the ancient city and wondered about their inhabitants. How had they lived? Where had they gone when the success and riches they'd found here ended? What had happened to them?

"Here he is." The relief in Nasir's voice was as obvious as the morning.

He came to his feet and ran forward. She turned her head just in time to see Ronu gallop out from behind a row of tall rocks.

He rubbed the animal's head as they greeted each other, grabbed the rope that hung from the saddle and rolled it up. "Saddlebag is gone. Probably got stuck somewhere and ripped off," he said.

"What was in it?" she asked.

"An old carpet for shade."

They would wish for that in a few hours, she thought, but was glad that he had had foresight enough to take the bag with their food and water into the well with them where everything had remained safe.

She stood and lifted that saddlebag, brought it to him.

He didn't attach it to the saddle, but pulled out one of the water bottles and dropped the bag onto the sand. "We should drink before we leave."

The bottle was small, enough for one good drink for two people. She was careful not to take more than half of it.

He took the bottle she handed him, but only drank a portion of his share. The rest he gave Ronu in his cupped palm. Then he took the saddle off the animal, rubbed him down while talking to him, gave him a handful of dried figs from the linen sack that held their food.

"I thought it over. I want to ride straight to Tihrin."

"Can we make it that far?" As far as she was concerned, the sooner they were out of the desert, the better.

"It's not that much farther. And there's a good well along the way," he said. "Umman's men will expect us to take the shortest way out. We might lose them if we go another route."

He knew his way around. She didn't. Her best chance for survival was to do as he said.

"Okay." She nodded, aware that he hadn't actually asked for her approval or opinion.

"Let's go." He saddled Ronu again as the camel lay on the sand before him.

He got on first and helped her up in front of him.

"Hang on," he said. "We need to go fast. I want to be out of sight before the trucks come back."

THE SUN WAS NEARING its highest point in the sky when Sadie spotted the walls of an enormous building. She twisted toward Nasir in the saddle, mindful that it had been a while since she'd spent this much time this close to a man. "Are we there?"

Hadn't he said they'd be going to some well? Had he changed his mind at one point and rode for some village after all? But the sleek towers and massive walls looked like no village she'd seen, and she'd been driven through a few on the way from the airport to the field hospital.

Hills of sand, mountains of it, stood to the

east. She could see no farther beyond them. In every other direction there was nothing but open desert. The place seemed abandoned, no animals, no people, not a tree or green thing anywhere.

Nasir was bringing Ronu to a halt, his attention focused completely on the buildings ahead, an odd expression on his face.

She tensed in response. "What's wrong? What is it?"

He watched and hesitated. "A legend," he said and set Ronu walking again, but kept a slow pace.

And as they got closer, she could see that it wasn't a city after all, but a single rambling palace, or rather a ruin of one, although amazingly well-preserved—much better than El Amarra.

"What legend?" She couldn't take her eyes off the row of domed roofs, the slim towers, the round-top windows

"There are legends about the pleasure palace of Mussafa Pasha somewhere near El Amarra. He controlled these territories at some point in the eighteenth century, toward the end of the Turkish rule. The last record of anyone having seen the place was over a hundred years ago."

She stared ahead at the impressive sight. How does something this big get lost? But before she asked the question, she came up with the answer on her own: sandstorms.

"We better get out of the sun." Nasir urged the camel into a trot.

She looked for some kind of doorway, but couldn't find any, just rows of evenly spaced windows. "The entrance must be on another side."

"The wind blew the sand off the top two floors only," he said.

Reaching the palace took longer than she'd thought. Distances in the desert looked shorter than what they were, an optical illusion, Nasir explained.

From afar, the building had looked impressive. Up-close, the beauty of the carvings that covered every inch of wall-space was breathtaking.

Nasir slid out of the saddle and helped her down, led Ronu on a rope as they stepped through a magnificent window.

"Wow," Sadie said as she took in the room.

Turquoise colored tiles decorated the bottoms of the walls, a repetitive pattern of painted tulips on top in a reddish color that was still intensely vibrant after hundreds of years. Sand covered the floor, probably a few feet deep, bringing the dark blue, star-speckled sky painted on the ceiling almost within reach.

Nasir was removing the saddle from Ronu. "We'll rest here until the air cools," he said and was already walking toward the doorway that led farther into the palace, leaving the camel behind.

She slipped off her headdress and shook the sand from it, making herself a little more comfortable, then followed him and found herself in some sort of hallway with evenly spaced openings that led to rooms similar to the one they'd just left behind, all lavishly decorated in different patterns.

"My brother and I spent a fair amount of time looking for this place in our younger years," Nasir said, walking a few feet in front of her. "Our grandfather was full of tales about it. They grabbed hold of our teenage imaginations." He glanced back at her with youthful excitement, looking like a different person from the one she'd known at the bandit camp.

So that dark intensity of his wasn't permanent. She risked a responding smile, thinking of the treasure hunts she'd used to have with her cousins, boys the both of them.

The thought of Nasir as a young boy, playing around in the desert with his brother, seemed to somehow make him less formidable, more real—unlike the dark warrior who commanded respect with a look, could kill with his bare hands and dove into quicksand to pull her out.

The farther into the palace they went, the higher the sand was on the floors, and the lower the ceiling. She slipped, but Nasir's arm shot out and steadied her, letting her go after a moment. Soon they reached a stone staircase that led to the palace's top floor. She followed Nasir up as he took the stairs with fluid grace.

Her chin just about dropped as she took in the large, circular room they'd come up in and its murals. The wall depicted a rolling meadow, going on and on all around them. But it wasn't the trees and the flowers in the grass that drew her attention. The meadow was populated by people—anatomically correct naked people—locked in various poses of passionate embrace. But despite the extremely explicit depictions, the painting was executed with such artistic skill and beauty that it could by no means be called pornographic.

The couple closest to her were making love in the shadow of a tree, the man's lips locked around the woman's breast as she threw her head back in ecstasy, their bodies poised at the point of joining. A gay little bee buzzed above them, a whimsical touch. The pleasure and urgent need on the woman's face seemed so real that Sadie felt her own body respond.

She looked away from them, but her gaze fell on the next couple, the man mounting the woman from behind as he caressed her front with peacock feathers. A handful of bees collected nectar from the flowers at their feet.

"I thought Islam forbids the depiction of

the human body in any form," she said without looking at Nasir when the silence between them grew uncomfortable.

He stood—well-built and darkly handsome like the men in the pictures—just a few feet from her. In the beginning she'd been aware of him as a threat, then in the last two days as an ally, counting on his skill and developing trust for him—but now in this place, for the first time, she felt aware of him as a man. And as far as men went, he was a fine specimen.

"The law wasn't always kept to the letter through the centuries," he said. "And there were always people who were powerful enough that they didn't have to keep it at all."

"What's up with the bees?" She glanced at the mural then back at him, aware that he watched her.

"According to the legend, Mussafa Pasha had a thing for honey," he said and smiled. His intense gaze that she'd often found threatening now burned with a different kind of heat.

She looked away, her attention falling on

the picture of the couple on the wall next to him. The woman was lying on her back, her spine arched toward the man, who had a bowl in one hand and a long-stemmed artist brush in the other. He seemed to have painted the woman's lips and breasts with a thick, golden substance she recognized now as honey. Shimmering swirls of it came to a peak on her swollen nipples.

The woman's knees were pulled up, her legs open wide, the joining of her thighs clean-shaven, her flesh parted. And into this crevice honey dipped from the brush, the man's head lowered, his tongue parting his lips a moment before reaching out to taste her.

Sadie stood rooted to the spot as Nasir strode toward her with measured steps, tall and strong and magnificently male. She wasn't scared, although she could not—or did not want to—name the odd sensation that skittered along her skin. The whole scene seemed unreal as if they themselves were part of some unlikely legend.

He stopped a short foot from her, his gaze skimming her hair, then coming to rest on her face. Heat swirled in his eyes. There seemed a sudden lack of air between them. She could not look away, nor could she move when he reached toward her.

She thought he might touch her face, but his fingers came, in a whisper-like caress, to the hair that curled around her ears. And then he seemed to catch himself.

"We should go back to the front so we can see if someone's coming," he said as he moved away. There was a hard set to his jaw now, betraying the effort his self-control required.

Then he walked by her, out the doorway and down the stairs. She took a deep breath and followed him, catching a glimpse, as she was leaving, of the picture of a man and a woman, doing things she would have thought impossible on the back of a camel.

Chapter Five

"This is Tihrin?" Sadie took in the sights, craning her neck. The rest of the ride through the desert had been long, and she was awed by the contrast of the bustling city.

Beharrain being the small country it was, she had expected a lot less of its capital… She couldn't think of what she had expected. What she found was a thoroughly modern metropolis.

Skyscrapers painted a breathtaking skyline, shopping malls and restaurants dotting the streets. Sprinkled among these were the most gorgeous old buildings, carved stone archways, brilliant tile work and sparkling domes.

The streets bustled with people. Street

vendors pushed their carts and loudly advertised their wares, men went about their business in suits that would have looked at home on Wall Street and women hurried along, some grasping the hands of their children. Most women wore the black *abayah,* their hair covered, although few had veils hiding their faces. Here and there, she even saw some uncovered heads, and spotted a couple of women in western dress, making her wonder if they were tourists.

They had left Ronu at a stable yard at the edge of the city where they'd cleaned up and Nasir had rented a car, which he now pulled up to the wrought-iron gates of the most splendid of the architectural wonders. He'd paid to make a phone call at the stable yard so she could call her mother and tell her she was safe. Since they were both crying too hard to make much sense, it had been a brief conversation.

If her mother could see this, she'd probably faint. Sadie stared at the palace in front of them. It was not the largest building she'd seen, but the most beautifully created.

One of the guards came over and saluted.

The ten-foot-tall gates swung open. She knew she was gawking, but she didn't care. It was her first time in a royal palace.

The courtyard they entered was blooming with hundreds of roses, grouped in an intricate pattern by color. Fountains spewed delicate streams high into the air. The sight of so much water after spending nearly two months in the desert was overwhelming. She wanted nothing more than to jump right in, but figured it wouldn't be appreciated by the guards.

Nasir parked the pickup just inside the gate. The door was opened for both of them before he even shut off the engine.

"Come," he said, and she kept pace.

Wherever they went, servants bowed to them, greeting Nasir with not only respect, but also with warm smiles. Yet Sadie couldn't relax. She couldn't forget that there were spies among them.

Nasir asked the pair of guards who flanked a set of gilded double doors something in Arabic—probably about his brother's whereabouts in the palace.

They gave an answer as they opened the door.

She was pretty sure she was about to meet

"His Majesty." Sadie glanced down at her *abayah.* Could have been cleaner.

"Nasir!" A little boy, about eight, started into a dead run at the other end of a long and richly decorated hallway coming toward them like a cannonball.

Nasir bent and absorbed the attack.

"Nasir! Nasir!" The squeals that came next were higher pitched, but just as powerful. Two little girls popped out of a doorway ahead to the left and ran into them full force, just about toppling Nasir.

He scooped up all three at once with a smile that transformed his face. The little girls giggled with abandon, the boy—probably since he was the oldest—tried to retain some semblance of decorum, but his eyes shone with joy, and admiration the kind of which Sadie'd seen kids his age carry for movie heroes.

"You protected your sisters while I was gone?" he asked the boy.

"Yes, Uncle."

"Well done." He nodded to his nephew with all seriousness, as one man to another.

A woman appeared next, strikingly

beautiful in an azure silk dress, the light of the crystal chandeliers glinting off raven-black hair that came to the middle of her back.

"Nasir." Her soft voice was thick with love as was the look in her dark eyes. She did not display her excitement like the children had, but it was clear she was equally glad to see him.

She was pregnant, at the end of her third trimester—judging by how low she carried.

"How was Paris?" she asked in English, and let her gaze, full of questions, slide over Sadie.

Nasir cleared his throat. "Let's talk about that later. How are you, Dara?" he asked, humor glinting in his eyes. "Does my brother ever have time to handle the affairs of the state? Looks like he's been busy in the royal quarters."

Dara laughed, a sound so seeped in happiness, Sadie felt a stab of sudden envy. So this was the American woman who had fallen in love with a king and came to live in his harem. It boggled the mind.

"Let me introduce Dr. Sadie Kauffman from Chicago."

"Oh." Her full mouth rounded in surprise. "I'm so pleased, Dr. Kauffman. I hope you will stay with us for a while. It would be such a pleasure to have you as our guest."

"Thank you," Sadie said and almost added, "Your Majesty," but it felt too weird.

"Please, call me Dara," the woman said, as if anticipating her unease.

The kids were still gripping Nasir, fighting over who could get closer to him, but their curious little eyes kept returning to Sadie.

"May I leave her to your care? I need to talk to Saeed." He jiggled them.

"Of course. He is in one of his conference rooms."

He started down the hallway, still carrying the kids, faking exaggerated lurches every couple of steps as if he were about to collapse, followed by delighted shrieks from his load.

Dara called after him. "It's good to have you back, Nasir."

"It's good to be here." He stopped and

glanced back for a brief second before leaving them.

Dara gave Sadie a speculative look. “I’m willing to bet my second-best crown you two didn’t meet in Paris. Come.” She turned and padded toward the magnificent door at the other end of the hallway. “I can’t wait to hear this.”

Sadie followed her, dazzled by the giant solid wood door at the end of the hall that was painted a gorgeous sky-blue with a gold pattern. It swung open silently as they approached. A maid was waiting on the other side. Dara asked for food and clothes to be brought to her rooms.

“Does everyone here speak English?”

“Most of the staff are bilingual,” Dara said.

Sadie relaxed a little further as she stared at the marble hallway ahead, the exquisite paintings on the walls, the vases dripping with exotic flowers. Arched entrances led to a multitude of rooms decorated with silk pillows, tiled walls that were works of art and sumptuous furniture.

Some of it reminded her of Mussafa’s

pleasure palace. Apparently Middle-Eastern architecture hadn't changed all that much in the past few hundred years, although the pictures here were mostly landscapes and portraits from the European masters. She stopped to browse the titles of several rows of antique volumes on a shelf.

"Now that I'm on bed rest with this little one—" the queen rubbed her belly "—I have more time for reading, and Saeed indulges me. The men of his family really do know how to spoil their women. You should hear the stories about his grandfather."

One of the rooms had the bathroom door open and as they passed, Sadie glimpsed a giant sunk-in pool in the middle. "Oh, wow."

Dara smiled. "It's one of my favorites. All this used to be guest quarters, but after we were married, Saeed had this whole wing redone for me and the children."

"So it's the harem?" Sadie looked around for signs of other women.

Dara laughed so hard she had to put up a hand to support her shaking belly. "I don't share. We really have a very normal family. Saeed and I…" She paused. "We were made for each other. Fate, you know?"

Sadie made some noncommittal sound. She didn't believe in fate.

"If he says I'm his one and only, then I'm his one and only," Dara added as she moved on. "Well, if he wants to live. Seriously, he doesn't take his word lightly. Nasir is the same." She gave Sadie another speculative look. "Here." She pushed a door open and led the way. "This is my American suite. Saeed had it made for me in case I ever felt homesick."

The room was decorated like an upscale American living room: a leather corner sofa, a big screen plasma TV in an antique mahogany armoir, the paintings on the wall all American landscapes.

"Not that my apartment in the U.S. ever looked like this," Dara said with a smile. "Saeed has a tendency to go overboard with his presents."

"Over there—" she pointed at one of the other doors "—is a bedroom. I thought it might be useful on those rare occasions when an old friend visits from the States. Of course, nobody ever uses it. Everyone always wants to stay in one of the more *exotic* suites."

She sat on the couch and motioned for Sadie to do the same. "So how did you two meet?" She tipped her head, her expression gracious, her smile warm, but her eyes sharp. "If you say the Louvre, I'm going to be very disappointed."

Sadie took a deep breath and decided to go with the truth. "I was a hostage in a bandit camp in Yemen, near the border."

"I hope you were not harmed." Dara's eyes filled with genuine concern.

Sadie shook her head. She had suffered, but it could have been much worse.

The maid came in with an armful of clothes on hangers; another woman behind her brought a giant tray of food.

"And Nasir rode to your rescue?" Dara asked after dismissing the women. She gestured to the tray. "Please, help yourself."

"Not really. He was one of the bandits," she said as she reached for a glass of pale juice.

"He couldn't be." Dara drew back, her friendly smile disappearing from her face as she went cold and defensive in the blink of an eye. "You must have misunderstood something," she said, looking every inch a woman standing up for her family, a woman not to be crossed.

For the first time, Sadie could see her as not just another American, but a formidable queen.

"He was undercover, looking for the old king, Majid," Sadie explained, not wanting her to take offense.

"Majid was there?" Surprise flashed across Dara's features.

Since Nasir came to the palace to tell his brother what he'd found at the bandit camp, Sadie figured it wouldn't do any grave harm for Saeed's wife to know the same.

"Toward the end, yes. He recognized Nasir. I think they were going to kill him." Having to think back to the camp brought a tightness to her chest.

Sadie forced a smile on her face and sipped her drink, waited until her racing heart settled, then she took a deep breath and told the whole story from beginning to end.

"So there are a spies in the palace?" Dara's face reflected no fear, only steely resolution.

"That's what Majid said to Nasir." Sadie bit into a piece of seasoned meat that had been rolled in sesame seeds, relaxed enough to eat, now that she was done with her story.

"They must be found." Dara came to her feet and paced. "I'm not going to have the enemy anywhere near my children."

"Now that the king knows, Nasir and he will find the men," Sadie said, not wanting to agitate her, and ate another piece of meat, followed by a slice of juicy sweet cantaloupe. "You shouldn't worry yourself."

Stress was bad in any stage of pregnancy. She'd seen plenty of cases where it had caused premature labor. As a doctor, her first instinct was to calm the woman in front of her who was already pressing a hand to her abdomen.

"Contractions?" she asked.

Dara shook her head with a distracted smile. "Kicking."

"You mentioned bed rest. Do you mind if I ask why?"

Dara paused.

"Occupational hazard." Sadie gave her an apologetic smile. "I can't help asking people personal questions about their health. It's a reflex. I didn't mean to pry."

Dara shook her head. "It's all right. I understand." She sank onto the couch. "I've had some bleeding."

"Recently?"

Dara nodded, and Sadie looked at her more carefully. Bleeding was not good news at this stage of gestation. *Placenta previa* and *placenta abruptio* came to mind. "You've been examined?"

"Exhaustively. I'm told everything looks fine."

"No dilatation?"

"Not yet, although God knows I'm ready." Dara smiled. "I can't possibly get any bigger than this."

Sadie flashed her reassuring physician smile. Even if there was some problem, the baby was fully developed at this stage—an important factor if it came to an emergency

C-section. And, of course, Dara would be getting superior care. "Make sure you get plenty of rest," she said.

"That's what my doctors said. I'm to spend as much time as I can flat on my back and worry about nothing."

"Excellent advice."

"I couldn't keep to it even before I found out about Majid."

"The palace guards seem capable," Sadie said.

"I appreciate your honesty. That you told me all this," Dara said after a while. "Saeed probably won't discuss it. He worries too much."

"Maybe he's right. Stress is—"

"If your children were in danger, wouldn't you want to know?"

She would. She wouldn't have made it as far as she had in her career without being a type-A, take-charge kind of woman.

"It comes down to who I really trust, doesn't it?" Dara said with a flat smile. "Not an easy question. Up to five minutes ago, I would have said *everyone.* Now, I'm thinking *no one.* No, that's not true. I trust

Saeed and Nasir, and their two sisters who are in France, studying at the Sorbonne. And I trust you. You haven't been in Beharrain long enough to be involved in this. And Nasir trusts you. He doesn't give his trust easily."

The vote of confidence felt good.

"If Nasir happens to mention anything to you about what he and Saeed are doing..." Dara drew her brows together.

"I doubt I'll see him much. Aren't unmarried men and women kept separate?"

"In general." Dara nodded. "Within the family's private quarters we are not as strict as that. We've been able to strike a good balance between Saeed's culture and mine."

"If I find out anything, I will let you know. But you have to promise not to worry about this. You need to rest."

"Mmm." The short, noncommittal sound was Dara's only response.

Judging by the look on her face, Sadie was pretty sure she was already making a plan.

NASIR DRANK another cup of spiced coffee and waited for the minister of trade to leave.

Then the door finally closed after the old man, and he was alone with his brother, the king.

"He's been in office for a long time," Nasir remarked. The man had become minister during their father's reign. When Majid had stolen the throne, he had replaced the majority of public officials with his own men. But not this one. Something to think about.

"Our father trusted him and so do I," Saeed remarked.

Nasir put down his cup and looked his brother in the eye. "Majid has spies in the palace."

"Of course there are spies in the palace," Saeed said after a moment of silence. He didn't seem the least disturbed. "There are spies in every palace."

"He's coming." Nasir stood his ground. "I saw him."

"And how many people were there by Majid's side?" Clearly Saeed was humoring him.

"About twenty. That's not the point—"

"For tonight, can we not put this aside

and celebrate the return of my brother from his much needed vacation in Paris?" The last word was said on a voice full of innuendo.

"I didn't go to Paris."

"No?" The look of shock on Saeed's face was rather exaggerated.

"If we were still boys..."

"You would have knocked me to the sand by now," Saeed finished the sentence. "It's nice to be king." He grinned.

"Don't mock me." Heat gathered in Nasir's belly. His patience had already been tried by the minister's presence. He'd been waiting for the past hour to get his brother alone.

Saeed leaned back in his chair. "Don't take Majid so seriously. He cannot harm us. He will be apprehended and sent back to prison."

"He deserves death. He killed our father." How was it that he was the only person who remembered that?

Saeed grew serious. "The courts decided. I cannot pursue revenge. Since I've taken the throne I've been asking people to forgive each other, to bond together to rebuild our country. I cannot do differently myself."

"Then use the law." He raised his voice, exasperated.

"I will. The ministry of justice will be notified of Majid's whereabouts. Thank you for that, although I wish you had not risked your life. You are much more important to us than whether Majid lives or dies."

Nasir's heated response died on his tongue, his throat tight all of a sudden.

They were interrupted by Dara before he could gather himself. The queen was popping her head in the door. "Where are Salah and the girls?"

"The nannies took them," Saeed responded. He got up and walked over, cupped his wife's face. "Shouldn't you be resting?"

"On my way." She brushed her lips against his briefly then gracefully ducked out.

"Why should she be resting?" Nasir's attention switched. He hadn't seen Dara rest a day since they'd known each other.

"She is having difficulties." Worry clouded

Nasir's face. "She's not supposed to be up for more than a few hours a day."

"And the doctors?"

"They are checking on her constantly."

Nasir nodded and relaxed. Over the years Dara had become like another sister to him, Saeed's children like his own.

"And your woman?" Saeed asked with an eyebrow arched.

Nasir paused. He hadn't mentioned that he'd arrived with a guest. One of the palace guards must have reported it. "She's not my woman."

"I understand she's not Beharrainian," his brother said.

"American."

Saeed nodded. "Dara will be happy for company." He paused before continuing, his gaze sharp on Nasir. "So how did you come to be in the company of this *friend?*" he asked, then added, "You realize, half the palace is already whispering you brought home a bride?"

"That's why I don't live at the palace. Everyone meddles."

"Mmm…" Saeed watched him. "I know

a sheik or two who wouldn't mind having you as son-in-law. I've been meaning to talk to you about this. I think—"

"I don't have time for this right now," Nasir cut him off.

"Of course, if your heart is set on the foreign woman." Saeed shrugged.

"No," Nasir said, and wished that the topic had never come up.

"Is she not beautiful?"

More than sunrise over an oasis. Not a discussion he was going to get into presently.

"She was a woman in danger and without protection," he said. "It was my duty to help her." He told Saeed how he found her, and what happened after.

His brother's face was dark by the time the story ended. "I will send out the troops."

"They are all over the southern desert. Majid is recruiting there heavily and in Yemen."

"Yemen? He wanted to occupy the northern region. Why would he have supporters there?"

"He is promising riches to men who

believe they suffer under the current government."

"Majid." Saeed said the single word with loathing.

He was starting to believe. Nasir leaned back in his seat and wondered where their cousin was now. He needed to get back into the desert, find the bastard and take care of him. But, for the first time that he could remember, Nasir felt reluctant to leave Tihrin and the palace.

He was concerned that Saeed wasn't taking the issue seriously enough, worried about his family having Majid's spies so close to them. "I will stay a while. Keep my eyes open, ask some questions, see if I can figure out who our enemies are inside the palace."

Saeed nodded. "There've been a few incidents."

"What incidents?"

"Papers that went missing from the offices. They are being investigated." He looked out a window for awhile. "I trust the guards and servants of the royal quarters. All are men known to me, all from our own tribe. I would guess Majid's men are among the lesser clerks."

Nasir nodded. He would start his investigation there.

"I would ask you not to mention this to Dara," Saeed said. "She is not allowed any stress. And sometimes—" he smiled "—she still thinks of herself as my bodyguard. If she knew something was amiss, she would want to help."

Nasir nodded. Dara wasn't likely to forget her military training. "We'll protect the women. It is better if they're not aware of anything."

"Exactly. We will catch the spies." A sudden smile lit Saeed's face, making him look ten years younger.

Nasir shook his head slightly. Governing a country must lack excitement. But he couldn't help grinning, too. He had missed his brother since Saeed had become king and moved to Tihrin permanently. "It's been a while since we have hunted together."

"Too long, brother."

Nasir nodded, satisfied with the outcome

of their talk. There was one more thing he wanted to tell his brother about. "Remember the legend of Mussafa's pleasure palace?"

Chapter Six

Nasir sat in the security office, struggling to keep awake. He had reviewed weeks' worth of security tape with the help of the chief of palace security. They couldn't find anything suspicious.

A large portion of the staff who worked in the royal quarters lived on site: the cooks, the maids, the nannies, the gardeners, the queen's personal chauffeurs and the like. The administrative staff commuted.

He found few instances of what could be construed as suspicious behavior. One of the cooks had a visitor who purposefully avoided looking at any of the security cameras, keeping his headdress on even in the palace, his chin down as he hurried in and out of the kitchen. One of the secretaries seemed to take home paperwork regularly. He would have to check if any of the employees had special authorization to work from home. The standard procedure was to prohibit any such activities for security reasons. Sensitive documents were much easier controlled if they never left the palace.

He came across a few clandestine meetings between clerks and maids from the royal quarters. They could have been lovers' rendezvous, or something far more sinister. Another thing to investigate. If he couldn't find anything to link them to Majid, there would be a few hastily arranged marriages.

"Anything else I can help you with?" Abbas came to him with that ready-to-die-for-you expression he normally wore only around Saeed.

The young man had been expelled from his own tribe for not backing down when the father of his beloved gave his daughter to another. Saeed had taken him in, given him a place in their camp, and ever since Abbas had been desperate to earn enough to eventually have a wife, even if not his first choice. Saeed had given him a job at the palace after he'd taken the throne.

"Found a wife yet?" Nasir asked.

"Two." Abbas grinned from ear to ear. "One in the city, one in Makresh."

Nasir nodded, knowing well the small village a few kilometers north from Tihrin. "There's nothing you can help me with here. Why don't you go home to one of them."

"No, Sheik Nasir. I cannot go while you work," he protested hotly.

"I'm sending you home." He didn't want him hovering, waiting on his next wish.

Abbas bowed deep, visibly distressed that he should be ordered away, but left at length. Nasir turned back to the computer and tapped his index finger on his desk. He was disappointed that the security tapes yielded so little. And he hadn't come up with much more on his own, although he'd been keeping his eyes and ears open. He couldn't shake the odd sense that he was watched and followed, although he couldn't pinpoint a single man. Saeed insisted that he was paranoid and had gotten unused to being in the palace. Servants *were* supposed to follow him and wait on him hand and foot. Maybe Saeed was right.

Nasir glanced over to the five security officers who were going through incoming and outgoing phone calls for the last three months. They had their work cut out for them. The digital recordings had been already scanned by computers to identify certain keywords they were looking for. Now they were listening one by one to the messages that had been flagged.

"There you are." Dara was coming through the door, a strained smile on her face. "I promised Sadie that I would show her the palace today, but the kids wore me out. Did you know Salah got into the armory? Anyhow, never mind that. Could you find some time to take Sadie around? She's been practically locked into my suites all day. Since she's leaving in a few days anyway…" Her voice trailed off as she watched him.

He glanced at the screen—plenty of work right here. But his eyes and brain were getting tired, fatigued enough that he might skip over something important.

"I'd be happy to take her to the Royal

Museum." Saeed and he had spent hours there when they were growing up.

"Oh, not that, that's not at all—" Dara fell silent.

He supposed she was right. To a woman, a western woman at that, the Royal Museum might not be terribly exciting. It was the pet project of the minister of defense and held little else than mementos of the country's most important battles. Dara had claimed a portion of one wing for Bedu artifacts. She wanted to make sure the Bedu way of life was amply recorded before it disappeared. She had adopted a number of causes like that since she had become queen, including the rehabilitation of war orphans and education for women. Her care for the country was deep and sincere. He loved her for that as much as he loved her for making his brother happy.

"I thought maybe the gardens on the roof," she said.

She was probably right. In her country, women liked flowers and long walks in parks. In his, there weren't nearly enough green things. People from the West often saw his country as bleak, too hot and too dry. Sadie would, too, he thought morosely. She probably hated it here. And how could he blame her? What had she seen so far, but the worst?

"I was going to show her the tent room, too," Dara said.

"I can do that." The tent room always made him feel at home. Would Sadie think it primitively exotic?

"I could have some sweets sent over," Dara went on.

Now that was a blatant bribe. They both knew she meant *Kishk El Fuara,* a pudding-like dessert, one of his few weaknesses.

The sweet, innocent look on Dara's face sent his instincts on high alert.

"The queen is amusing herself this morning by playing matchmaker, is she?" He watched her closely. He had to remember that Dara had been in the military. She was an excellent strategist.

The way she'd hurried from breakfast, claiming fatigue and leaving him alone with Sadie—his brother had gone off to a meeting already—gained new meaning all of a sudden.

"Wouldn't dream of it." She smiled. "Saeed is looking forward to negotiating a Bedu bride for you. He's been whittling down the list of sheiks with eligible daughters."

"He wouldn't." Saeed would have told him, wouldn't he? Surprise and irritation played tug-of-war with Nasir, then he remembered that Saeed *had* breached the subject, but he hadn't been willing to listen.

Dara tilted her head. "You have been of age for a long time. He is the oldest man in your immediate family. I understood this was your custom."

And *he* understood that Saeed was going to leave him alone. Nasir swallowed his sudden swell of annoyance. He had thought of taking a wife when he'd been twenty-two, but the girl had died shortly before the wedding, killed by an infection that had not been taken seriously until it was too late.

From time to time, he had thought of offering for someone else, but his intentions had never been carried out. He'd been too involved in setting up an uprising to get his brother back on the throne. And since Majid had disappeared from prison, Nasir had spent all his energies on finding the bastard.

He'd forgotten lately that as sheik, he was expected to marry, for the tribe's sake as much as his own. His marriage would strengthen his tribe's alliances. Apparently his brother remembered that more readily than he did.

"Anyone in particular?" he asked, and although he had always been perfectly content to carry on tradition, now he found the idea oddly uncomfortable.

"Sheik Omar ibn Muhammad has eleven daughters, as I understand."

Did he? Nasir tried to think of his most recent visit to that tribe. He hadn't noticed. His mind had been on finding Majid.

"There are others," Dara said. "I can't remember the names. Every time I am pregnant I feel like I get hormonal brain damage." She smiled apologetically.

He barely heard her. All he could think of was that Saeed had a horde of women lined up for him and never bothered to mention anything. "So how long has my brother been plotting behind my back?"

"He hasn't been plotting. People come to him. You're the most eligible bachelor in the country. Then you come to the palace with Dr. Kauffman, the two of you alone, and naturally everyone assumes..." Her voice trailed off as she watched him speculatively.

"Everybody should mind their own business," he said, and it occurred to him that he knew Sadie better than he would know the woman he would someday marry. She was smart, a doctor, as courageous as a warrior—she had saved his life at the bandit camp—and she had beauty enough to steal a man's heart at one glance.

As sheik, he would be expected to choose from the daughters of other tribal leaders. He would visit the man's tent, catch a few glimpses of a girl, as much as he could with her body, hair and face covered. If he were serious and came back a second time, they might be allowed to speak a few words with her family present. The next time he would see her would be after their wedding, which she would not attend. In the Arab world weddings were little more than contracts, agreed upon by the men of the two families. The two sexes would celebrate separately. He would not be able to speak a private word, nor see his wife's face, until their wedding night.

Saeed had always been the progressive brother between the two of them, Nasir the one who kept to the Bedu ways and fought ceaselessly to preserve tradition. And yet now, at least in this matter, he suddenly found tradition insufficient.

Dara was smiling at him, moving toward the door. What did she have to be so happy about?

"Thank you for helping me out with Sadie. I better get to bed. The doctor will be looking for me to do a checkup," she said.

As morose as he felt, he forced a smile on his face. His worry over Saeed not taking the threat to his throne seriously and his frustration with not yet having a clue to the identities of the spies was getting to him. None of which was his sister-in-law's fault.

"Take care, Dara."

When she was gone, he signed off the computer, planning on returning for an hour or two later that night. A small break, a little walking around was just what he needed to refresh his brain so he could finish this batch of video files.

He got up and stretched his shoulders, talked to the security chief, then walked upstairs to the royal quarters and paced the central foyer while he waited for Sadie. He used the time to go over everything he had found that day, to examine each new clue from every possible angle.

Then he heard the soft sound of shoes on the marble floor and he looked up. His brain stopped in midthought. By Allah, if Dara had hidden motives as he suspected, she sure knew how to bring out the heavy artillery.

Sadie floated toward him in a long silk dress the color of golden desert sand. While the material modestly covered her body, the dress was tailored in such a way that it hinted at all the pleasures of the seven heavens, tantalizing with every step she took.

Women did not wear the *abayah* or cover

their hair and face when at home, not even in the most traditional households, and Saeed's had been much reformed since Dara's arrival. Nasir had gotten used to seeing Dara dressed freely in Western attire. Sadie, however, was not his relative, although he had taken her under his protection.

"Hope you've been enjoying your day." His voice came out strained. He hadn't seen her since that morning's meal, and he realized now all of a sudden how very long ago that had been.

"I've been keeping company with Dara. She was telling me about the country's history and your family. It's fascinating. Did you know Salah got into the armory?" She shook her head, her short golden hair swinging around her nape.

"I've heard." There were few places Salah hadn't gotten into. The boy was currently preparing to be an explorer. A step up from last year's career choice of pirate. He had a rough time accepting that becoming the terror of the high seas was an entirely unsuitable and disreputable occupation for a prince. Then again, his great-grandfather had led caravan raids, actually stole his bride from one, and he'd been king.

"Is everything all right?" Sadie was watching him.

"Just thinking about how times change," he said and turned. "Let's start with the gardens."

NASIR in the traditional robe and dress of his people was darkly handsome. Nasir in a suit was a two-legged cardiac arrest. Sadie tried not to gawk as she caught up with him.

The Western clothes seemed to close the distance between them somehow. He could have been any of her neighbors back at home, any of the doctors at the hospital. Well, not *any,* really. She hadn't ever met anyone quite like him.

Had he been offended by the exotic dress Dara had insisted she should have? The odd look he'd given her was hard to interpret. It was a fine dress, though, no matter what anybody thought. The cool silk caressed her skin with every step, the loose fit comfortable in the heat of the evening. And it did seem suitably modest, at least by Western standards. The hemline came to her ankles and the long, flowing sleeves covered her arms to the wrist. The neckline was as prim as could be. She was as well-covered as if she wore the *abayah,* although the dress' fine material, lovely color and flattering cut were a far cry from that shapeless, drab garment.

They engaged in small talk as he led her up a curving staircase carved from stone, chatted about what she thought of the queen's quarters, if she'd had enough rest.

Then they finally reached the gardens and whatever his last polite question had been was promptly forgotten.

She could do nothing but stare.

Paradise.

Or as close to it as man could come.

"It's stunning," she said, finding the word insufficient.

Palm trees bobbed in the evening breeze, grass—honest to goodness grass—edged the bricked walkway. The profusion of flowers was dizzying, their colors and scents a true feast for the senses.

"It seems unreal." She moved forward as the garden drew her in.

The balmy air on her face felt wonderful. She'd spent the day with Dara, even took lunch in the queen's quarters. She'd been pampered to death and received a new wardrobe. And they talked ceaselessly about everything from Dara's life in Beharrain to Sadie's misery at the bandit camp.

"My grandmother planted the first garden up here," Nasir said. "My father made sure it was tended after her death, but during the civil war and Majid's rule the plants were neglected and most of them died. Dara has been working on restoring the garden based on old pictures."

She's doing a fabulous job, Sadie thought. From everything she'd seen so far, Queen Dara seemed happy and fulfilled—not at all what she would have expected from a Western woman in this situation. She'd thought Dara was trapped here by her love for the king, willing to give up her own culture. But the woman she'd gotten to know that afternoon appeared anything but "trapped." She ruled. And nobody could deny that she looked radiantly happy.

The garden's beauty drew Sadie's attention from the enigma of the queen. The winding path before her begged to be explored. She heard water somewhere just around the corner. She discovered the source once they rounded the bend—a magical fishpond with a cleverly sculpted waterfall. She watched the silver fish play in the moonlight, then caught sight of the night sky reflected in the water. The millions of stars drew her gaze up.

"It's incredible." The night had a dreamlike quality.

"Breathtaking," Nasir said behind her, and he didn't even have full view of the pond since she was standing right in front of him.

She stepped aside. "I didn't realize anything like this could exist in the desert."

"Have you ever heard of the Hanging Gardens of Babylon?"

"One of the seven wonders of the ancient world," she said. That was the extent of her knowledge.

"The gardens were built by King Nebuchadnezzar. The story goes that he married Amyitis, daughter of the king of the Medes, to create an alliance between the two nations." A shadow crossed Nasir's face, disappearing as he went on with the story. "Apparently she was used to a more mountainous and green country and became homesick in arid Mesopotamia. Besotted by love, the king built her a giant hill of terraced gardens with trees and flowers, watered constantly from the Euphrates River."

"Maybe your grandfather built the gardens inspired by that story."

He nodded. "My grandmother was English. I suppose she missed seeing all that green. My grandfather had the roof prepared and set up the irrigation system, imported the trees and flowers. But she insisted on directing the planting and putting her hands in the dirt alongside the servants."

Dara had told her the wild story of the king's grandmother having been kidnapped from a caravan during a raid. If the beauty she had created was any indication, she must have been extremely happy here.

They moved on from the pond and down the path, found themselves at an alcove. White roses glowed in the moonlight, covering an ornate stone arch that had a marble bench beneath it. There was writing carved into the arch.

"What does it mean?" she asked.

He paused for a moment. "Love," he said, then added, "but more than that. I don't know if your language has a word for it. It's love beyond measure."

Love beyond measure. She wondered what that was like, if it existed outside this enchanted garden where everything seemed possible. In her experience, romantic love was, at best, conditional, and always temporary.

"Would you like to sit?" he asked, his voice as thick as the perfume of the flowers that surrounded them.

She looked at how small the bench was, made for lovers, and felt nervous all of a sudden, scared. Not of him, but of the awareness of him she didn't seem to be able to shake. He was like the garden by moonlight, a complex pattern of light and shadow that drew her to discover more.

"I sat all day," she said too quickly, and moved away.

They walked on quietly for a while, then came upon a sculpture garden and she forgot the awkward moment between them. Richly carved arches of granite and columns with stone flowers so delicate they appeared real in the moonlight dotted this corner of the roof.

"I've never seen anything like this," she whispered in awe.

"Some of them are almost a thousand years old," he said.

After she looked her fill, they walked on. He let her set the pace, always following a step behind.

"Do you mind?" She stopped at the edge of an area where the grass widened.

"Do as you wish."

She slipped out of her silk slippers and stepped on the grass, smiled from ear to ear at the childish pleasure of it. "I didn't realize how much I missed lawn." Not that she'd walked barefoot over it a lot lately. Not since she'd been a child. Her condo in Chicago was on the seventh floor, the building surrounded by road and parking lots.

Instead of making fun of her as she had

half expected, he stepped out of his shoes and socks and joined her. Then, after a moment of thinking, he took off his suit jacket and tie, tossed them on the grass.

"Western clothes are not very practical outside of the air-conditioned parts of the palace," he said as he unbuttoned the neck of his shirt first then the sleeves to roll them up.

She glanced away from the muscles of his forearm and moved forward. The neatly clipped grass tickled the soft skin between her toes as she meandered under the palm trees, all the way to the edge of the roof to lean over the three-foot stone wall.

The courtyard and its roses spread below them, the fountains still going. She wished she could capture this moment of beauty somehow and take it with her, have it forever.

She must have made some kind of noise, maybe sighed, because Nasir asked, "Do you miss your home?"

The question startled her. She hadn't thought about home all day. As a general idea, yes, she missed it, but it was hard to put anything specific behind that. The home she'd grown up in had been sold long ago. The house her mother now lived in was a place for Sadie to visit, but held no strong attachment. And Chicago… "The life I left," she said. "It's kind of over. I'm not going back to it." Although she wasn't sure just what she wanted to do next.

He was looking at her, puzzled, and she felt compelled to explain, although she wasn't sure if her thoughts would make sense to anyone else but her. "It's different here. Time is different. I mean, there is time. At the camp, it was terrible, but I had time to think about who I was, what this life was that I was about to lose, all the things I've never done. I was thinking, oh, my God, I'm never going to see the world and skydive and learn to ski and get married and have a child. And then I realized that even if I hadn't been kidnapped, even if I wasn't killed by the bandits, most likely I wouldn't have had those things anyway. The life I set up for myself, my career, didn't leave room for anything else."

"So what's next?" He looked at her as if

he understood her and didn't think she'd gone soft in the head.

"I don't know," she admitted. "I want to live. I want to work, but sometimes I want to just walk in a garden like this, or sit in the desert and watch the sun rise." She wanted what Dara had; the thought came out of the blue and surprised her. What *did* Dara have? A loving husband, children, the opportunity to make a difference. It wasn't the palace she envied—she wasn't sure she could ever get used to the splendor. But she wanted to be happy like Dara was, to find that true happiness that came from the bones and radiated out through the skin and lit up the eyes.

"What do you want from life?" she asked and realized how unusual that question was, not something she'd ever asked from any of her colleagues at the hospital, where relationships were too superficial and competitive to go beyond small talk. And yet, she felt comfortable asking Nasir.

"To protect the ones I love," he said without thinking. "I want my people to have a chance."

The answer was straightforward and noble like the man. He stood straight and tall, looking rather heroic in the moonlight. He was as still as the night, and it occurred to her that he rarely rushed. He had a tribe to lead, a heritage to save, spies to catch and here he was with her in the garden, sharing a timeless moment.

"I think in my world there's too much pressure to achieve all we can as fast as we can. The whole *he who dies with the most toys wins* thing, you know? And here, it's like you are more than just your own life. The desert is the same as it was five hundred years ago and five hundred years from now it will still be here. Each life is a link in a chain and it's the chain that matters."

Surprise flashed across his face and something else she couldn't quite interpret. "You understand," he said, his eyes bottomless wells in the darkness.

The fountains below them switched patterns, the splashing water making a new kind of music. The beauty of the night was intoxicating. All of her senses were alive and alert. When Nasir turned toward the half wall next to her and leaned his elbows on it, his nearness was like a touch.

She heard his intake of breath as he prepared to say something, but then he stopped, and she saw what interrupted him.

Someone was scurrying across the palace yard below, keeping in the shadows. The man paused, looked around, then disappeared behind one of the doorways.

ALI IBN SALEH. Nasir recognized the man when he turned his head as he stepped through the door.

"Who is that?"

"A man on his way to a woman he has no business seeking in the middle of the night, no doubt," he said with a shrug.

He was head of the royal stables, which were nowhere near the palace yard. He would have a talk with Ali later tonight. Until then, the cameras should record if he tried to enter any sensitive areas.

"Would you like to see the throne room?" he asked and went back to put his socks and shoes on. The security offices were located near there. He could pop in and pass on what he'd seen.

"I'd love to," she said and turned in the moonlight, her short hair swinging around her ears.

She looked unreal, an enchanting desert spirit, as she reached for her silk slippers.

He led the way down through another staircase, through one of the many salons, across the pink marble hall and to the throne room finally, where the guards opened the doors for them without questions.

"What do they do here?" She was looking around wide-eyed.

"Not much. Celebrating important state occasions and receiving other royalty and presidents. Mostly it's a waste of space. Prince Salah once asked if it could be turned into a roller skating rink." He shook his head. "I think Dara was telling him stories from her childhood."

She remained silent. The crystal chandeliers, fifteen-foot-tall mirrors and the pink marble floor tended to have that effect on first time visitors.

"Do you mind if I step out for a moment?"

"No. Of course not. If you have to work, or need to be somewhere else—" Dara said.

"I have time. I'll be back in a second."

She nodded.

He left her to admire the painted ceiling that she seemed to just now discover. The security office was down the hall. He went straight to the chief, who would be there all night tonight, and every night while they were on high alert.

"Ali ibn Saleh," he said. "I want him followed, but not approached." There were plenty of areas that were not watched by cameras. He wanted to know the man's every move.

"Yes, sir." The chief passed on the order at once.

"If you find anything suspicious, you can report to my cell phone. I won't be far," Nasir said, and gave the man the location of the door where he'd seen Ali disappear then he hurried back to Sadie. He found her in the back, looking at a Persian rug that was over five hundred years old.

"I've never seen anything like it," she said.

"Would you like to explore more of the palace?"

"I feel like I'm in a dream." She nodded. "All this can't possibly be real."

He was beginning to feel the same. What in Allah's name was he doing wearing a suit and strolling through the palace with a beautiful foreigner? At this time last week he'd been hunting traitors in the desert.

"What would you like to see next?" he asked.

"Dara said something about a tent room."

He bit back a smile. His sister-in-law was nothing if not thorough.

"As you wish. Many well-to-do businessmen and nobility have tent rooms in their homes," he explained as they made their way to their destination. "You have to remember, just two or three generations ago, we were mostly nomads. Oil built our cities fast, changed people, but there hasn't been enough time to forget."

"What was it like before?"

"Better," he said on instinct then modified it with a smile. "At least, I like to think.

Right was right. The Bedu code meant something. People were more honest."

"It was probably quieter," she said. "More peaceful."

"Maybe quieter. As for peaceful, my grandfather had a lot of tales about raids and wars. But it was Bedu, you know? The foreigners changed everything."

"The money, you mean?"

"They brought a lot more than money." He paused. "All through the desert there were tribes, trading, raiding, raising sheep and goats and camels, running caravans. They fought over wells and territories from time to time, but all in all life was in balance."

She nodded, and he went on.

"Then foreigners came and the oil was found. And they said to one tribe, 'Look, you have this black stuff under the sand. You can't eat it, your camels can't eat it. You have no use for it. Give it to us and we'll give you more powerful weapons to defeat your enemies.'"

She was silent, listening.

"Then the killing began. More money

came, better weapons. By the time it was over, our people were deeply divided, and the oil rights belonged to foreigners who were practically running the country." He didn't bother to keep the bitterness out of his voice.

"All foreigners are not like that," she said after a while.

"No. But for a long time, those were the only foreigners we saw here, people who either came to steal or to conquer. The simple people didn't understand that when unethical corporations contaminated tribal grazing grounds and wells, they weren't here at the direct order of their governments and with their countries' full knowledge and approval."

"But it has nothing to do with me, the rest of us." She sounded frustrated.

Good, she understood then how he felt. "As I and the rest of my people have nothing to do with the bandits and terrorists. We are more. We have scientists, architects and poets. We love peace. We want to see our children grow up as much as you do." He fell silent for a moment before he said, "But *you* know that. You came to help."

"I didn't," she said and looked embarrassed. "I came so I could get a promotion when I got home."

"But it's different now." He looked at her and at that moment felt as if he could see straight to her soul. "The desert changed you."

She nodded.

He believed her, although, until now, he'd been sure the desert talked to none but the Bedu. "You were meant to come."

She opened her mouth to say something, but they had reached the tent room and he pushed the door ajar, and whatever she was about to tell him was forgotten.

She blinked. "This is not like your tent at the bandit camp."

He had to smile at that. "It's a royal tent."

The floor was covered with priceless carpets, richly woven pillows thrown on top of those, red and white, the colors of his tribe.

A laden tray of sweets—*baklava, Kishk El Fuara* and *halva*—waited for them on a low copper table, next to it a graceful pitcher of honeyed jasmine tea.

"I like it," she said as she looked around. "Some of the palace… It's a little too much for me take in. I don't know how Dara ever got used to it. I slept in the American Suite last night. But this place…" she said as she sank onto an oversize pillow, "it seems strange, but I feel comfortable here."

"Me, too," he said, although the hard tile floor under the carpets was a far cry from the softness of the desert sand. He never felt half as at home anywhere as he did in a Bedu tent.

He sat on the pillow next to hers and poured them both a drink.

"Thank you. What are these?" She gestured toward the tray.

He explained each dessert.

"I've had *baklava* before. I'll try the other two." She popped a piece of *halva* into her mouth and her eyes rounded as she made a small sound of pleasure.

He looked away and tried hard to focus on the cup in his hand.

"This could be addictive," she said, then

a moment later followed up with a question. "Do you live in the palace?"

Allah forbid. "I think it's the first time I've spent a night here since the coronation. I mostly stay with my *fakhadh* in the desert."

"Does that mean your tribe?"

"A small part of my tribe. No place has enough water and grass to support a whole tribe. Most of the Bedu live in large families. My *fakhadh* is a group of my closest male relatives and their wives and children."

"You don't mind being so far from everything?"

"The Bedu are my people, the desert is my home. What you see as inconvenience, I see as freedom. It is dear to me."

"No, not inconvenience," she said. "That morning we spent at the ruins of El Amarra, I felt like I could stay there forever." She fell silent for a moment. "It's like—You'll laugh. But when we were crossing the desert, I felt like there was something more there, something the eye couldn't see. I was scared witless, but even through that I could see such beauty."

A feeling of lightness surrounded his heart. He squelched it. What did it matter if Sadie thought she could come to like the desert or not. In a few days, she would be gone.

And the thought, even though he had understood that was how it would be all along, snapped something in him and brought out the uncivilized man he'd been fighting to keep hidden.

Who was she to share this evening with him, these moments, to sit in this tent with him alone and look like she did and smile like she did and expect him to let her walk away?

"Be careful of the desert," he said as he set his cup down. "They say it sings to you. They say once you hear its song, you can never leave it."

And then he kissed her.

Chapter Seven

Oh, thank God, Sadie thought. The awareness between them all evening had been driving her crazy.

The way he had looked at her up on the roof… She would see that burning, dark gaze in her dreams for the rest of her life. The small, logical part of her that came in so handy at work knew that most of the magic between them came from the magic of the night itself, from the beauty he had shown her, from Dara's efforts to get them to spend time together, her own confused feelings, her gratitude. The rest of her didn't care.

She never wanted the night to end.

His lips tasted of honey from their tea, bringing to mind images from Mussafa's pleasure palace. Desire, sharp and urgent, flooded her body and she pressed against him. With a muffled groan, her host for the evening, the impeccably polite and restrained businessman who wore a suit, was gone. The man for whom she opened her lips was a wild desert warrior.

He mastered her. There was no other word for it.

Her nerve endings danced to the rhythm of his heartbeat under her palm as her hand glided across the muscles of his chest. He caressed her through the silk, long, slow strokes down her back that had her spine tingling and a low sound of desire escaping her throat. He deepened the kiss and pulled her to him, roughly, with need. Then he seemed to catch himself. He pulled his body back an inch or two and cupped her face gently, finished the kiss with so much tenderness, it constricted her throat and left her bewildered.

"I must apologize," he said when he drew back. "It is not the custom of my people to act like this."

How on earth was she supposed to respond?

"If you were Beharrainian, I would have to marry you now," he said with a flat smile.

"For that?"

"For less than that." He held her gaze.

Oh, no, he couldn't keep looking at her like this. They both knew where that led. She was not in Tihrin to engage in a brief affair with some sheik. She needed to recover from her desert ordeal and fly right back to the States.

"The fault is mine," he said as he stood.

"We both..." She couldn't finish the sentence. Lost their heads? Thought with their hormones? What?

But he seemed to understand and nodded. "You are an exceedingly wise and stunning woman," he said as if in his defense. "I had not known what true desire was before I met you."

Oh, God. She couldn't look at him, just couldn't. They were alone in an enormous, lustrous tent, with dozens of pillows scattered at their feet, luxurious fabrics, silky softness. The place was like a movie set—

incredible in its beauty, irresistibly romantic and sensuous.

"I will walk you back to the queen's quarters." His voice was rich with barely restrained passion.

It wasn't real. None of it was real, she kept reminding herself as she nodded and followed him. The night had been set up by the queen so Sadie would have an opportunity to find out how Nasir and Saeed were doing with their investigation. Take away the palace, the gardens and the tent, the exotic magic of it all and they would have nothing left but two strangers who barely knew each other, who didn't even share a common culture.

Still, she could not deny the chemistry. To be fair, she had to admit they had that.

She would just have to get over it. She was going to start a fabulous new life when she got home, a life that would matter, one that brought her joy and made a difference to others.

They walked together to the doors of the queen's quarters.

"Any luck figuring out who Majid's spies

are?" she asked nonchalantly at the last minute.

"None," he said, seeming preoccupied. Then he said a polite good-night as he opened the door for her.

Sadie hadn't gotten anything that she could pass on to Dara. Except...the man down in the courtyard. He *had* acted suspicious.

"Good night." She stepped through the threshold, and when the door closed behind her, stayed where she was.

After a few minutes, she peeked outside, paying no mind to the guard. The hallway was clear. Excellent. She slipped out and moved with a purpose. She remembered roughly which door that strange man had slipped behind.

She couldn't just tell Dara that she'd seen some man go in some door. At the least, she had to find out where the door led. The queen then could take that information to her husband or to security if she thought it was relevant.

She'd go down to the courtyard and through that door to see if it led to the kitchens or offices or what. It would take no more than ten minutes and give her some specific information, plus it would give her something to do other than obsess over that kiss. God, what a kiss it had been. Her body and mind were still reeling.

The courtyard was eerie and unguarded save the security cameras. There were several checkpoints before this area of the palace. Sadie was allowed to pass each, the advantage of being the queen's guest.

She kept to the shadows, her nerves frayed. She wasn't a spy, for heaven's sake, she wasn't cut out for secret missions in the middle of the night. Not that she planned on entering any kind of confrontation. All she wanted was to find out where the man had gone, perhaps who he was. If she saw him again, she could point him out to a servant and ask.

She could see the row of doors across the courtyard, over a dozen of them. Which was the right one? She glanced up and found the garden on the roof, the palms she thought they'd been standing under when they'd seen the man. *Let's see…* She picked one of the doors and was fairly sure she had picked correctly. The lights were on behind it.

As far as she could tell, the staff never slept. When she'd woken up in the middle of the night to go to the bathroom and turned the light on, a maid immediately appeared to ask her if she needed anything.

There had to be servants here, too. The thought gave her some comfort as she moved forward. She would gain the information she needed then take it back to Dara. Let her make what she wanted of it.

Something in the corner of the courtyard caught her attention. An ornately formed bush moved. She stopped and held her breath, flattened her body to the wall, at once questioning the wisdom of having come down here by herself in the middle of the night. There might have been a horde of people in the building ahead, but out here, right now in the dark, she was alone.

The bush moved again, and not from any breeze. The air stood still in the closed courtyard.

Who was there?

She watched, rooted to the spot, as a man

in a dark suit stepped forward. Then she recognized the graceful power in the man's movements—Nasir.

She opened her mouth to call his name. He had to be here after the same guy. They might as well continue together. Her little mission didn't seem as tame now as she'd originally thought. The man in the bushes could have just as easily turned out to be somebody else, someone with bad intentions, even the man she'd seen earlier who, if he was a spy, wouldn't take kindly to being followed. But before she could call out to Nasir, a small pop disturbed the silence of the night.

What was that? She glanced around and saw a shadow move behind a half-open window.

"Nasir." She whispered a warning, but she was too late.

Nasir was on the ground.

From the way he lay—on his side, clutching his chest—it was obvious he hadn't just ducked for cover.

"Guard!" she shouted at the top of her lungs, knowing something was drastically wrong. She lurched forward, glancing to the window again, but the shadow was gone. "Somebody, help!"

"Stay back," he said as she reached him.

She could hear him wheezing as he tried to come to his feet.

"Lie down." She gently pushed him back to the pavers and eased his blood-soaked shirt open to get a look at his injury.

She found a small entry wound in the left side of his chest, too high to have hit the heart. She pressed her hand against the hole and turned him, ripped his shirt to check for the exit wound. She found it, thank God.

"The bullet is out," she said, calmer now.

She had assessed the situation, knew what she had to do, would not let the desperate sound of him gasping for air distract her, make her panic.

When his chest expanded, the air went in through the holes, filling his chest cavity instead of going through his windpipe to fill up his lungs.

She pressed her left palm firmly against the exit wound in his back and laid him on it, then pressed her right hand against the entry hole in his chest. "Breathe in," she ordered.

He did.

She watched his chest rise as his lungs expanded.

She removed her right hand and opened the hole. "Breathe out."

His movement expelled air not only from his lungs but his chest cavity as well. Blood came, too. Nothing but clean blood. Maybe his lung hadn't been hit.

She pressed her palm back into place. "Breathe in."

She repeated until the first of the guards got there, then the royal physicians with their fancy emergency kits. Then came the royal ambulance, handily kept at the palace.

She ignored the doctors' disapproving glances and got in the back with them, fighting the urge to shove the men back and take care of Nasir herself. But the doctors were competent; she couldn't find fault with a thing they did.

If she hadn't been there... A few minutes and his chest cavity would have filled with blood. Another few minutes and his brain would have shut down from lack of oxygen. Then he would have been gone.

Nasir turned his head toward her. "You saved my life again," he said, his voice weak.

"I had to." She kept her voice light, made an effort to wipe the worry off her face. "You saved mine a few times. I owe you."

He nodded soberly, his dark gaze burning into hers. "Our lives belong to each other."

NASIR DID NOT remain the only patient in the royal wing of the hospital. He was still in surgery when the ambulance came in again with the king himself.

"Saeed was shot!" Dara hurried down the hall, grim determination on her face. "When they find the bastard I'm going to rip his heart out. The coward shot him through a window."

She was stopped politely but firmly at the door of operating room number two, accepted the doctor's orders after some bristling and let Sadie help her to a chair, refusing to go to the plush royal suite upstairs.

"Lean back. You need to calm down. He'll be fine." Sadie rubbed her back to ease the knotted muscles. "Where was he hit?"

"In the heart." The last word came out on a sob as Dara pushed to her feet. "I can't stand waiting around. I want to go back and lead the palace search."

"You won't." Sadie stood, too, to push her down to the chair again. She had stayed outside, not wanting to interfere with the surgical team. She wasn't a surgeon; she would have only been underfoot. Still, as a doctor, it killed her not to be there.

Dara sat. "We'd just received news of Nasir and were getting dressed to come to see him."

"Someone shot at him, too. Didn't hit anything vital. I was right there."

"Thank God. Thank God." Dara jumped up, caught herself and sat down again. "Simultaneous attacks," she said. "Majid's spies."

Sadie nodded, having come to the same conclusion. "They didn't succeed. The king and his brother are both alive." And now that they were in the operating room, hopefully they would stay that way. "The children?"

"Safe with their nannies, under the protection of the royal guard in a reinforced section of the palace. There'll be a large scale attack soon," Dara said. "We have to prepare now. Whether the assassins succeeded or not, Majid will use this momentum. The people will be worried. They'll think Saeed's rule is weakening. Those who were on the fence before will be even more reluctant to commit their support to the king now."

She took a deep breath and straightened, visibly pulling herself together. "Majid will start the fighting in a few days. He'll wait that long to hear if the assassins succeeded, for the news to get out and spread." She turned to the guard who came with her. "I need to get the minister of defense on the phone."

"What can I do to help?" Sadie asked.

"Stay with me." Dara took a deep breath and blew it out, then put a hand to her belly. "I think the baby is coming."

MAJID LEANED BACK onto his pillows and smiled. *Al hamdu lillah!* Praise God. "The news is confirmed?" he asked the messenger who stood before him, his eyes cast to the carpets.

"Yes. Both lost a lot of blood—Saeed the worst. He is not expected to live to see morning."

Hearing those words was a balm to his soul.

Saeed and Nasir were out of the way, his path to the throne clear. He'd been careful that nothing would connect the assassins to him.

A mob was arranged to attack the palace in four days, once the news of the king's demise reached even the last Bedu camp. There would be chaos. Religious fanatics who had never accepted the Western woman at their king's side would now turn viciously against the whore. Who knew, she might die when the palace was attacked. Yes, that would be best, preferably before she gave birth to another one of her bastards.

The heir, though, the firstborn son from Saeed's first wife, a Muslim woman, must stay alive. Orphaned at eight and at the head of the country in turmoil, the poor boy. And

Majid his closest adult male relative. He would save Salah and help him rule. And if the boy met with some unfortunate accident a year or two from now, nobody would question Majid's stay on the throne. After all, he had held the position before.

THE NIGHT of the assassination attempts and the day that followed passed in a blur of activity.

Prince Aziz ibn Saeed emerged into the world around noon, a healthy little boy at four kilos and thirteen decagrams. About nine pounds two ounces, Sadie figured.

She'd spent the night running from Saeed's operating room to the recovery room Nasir occupied, then to delivery where Dara needed her support to help her through a difficult labor. She kept an eye on the doctors and nurses, made sure everything they did was necessary and properly done. Did Majid have people at the hospital as well as at the palace? Was there someone here, even now, who might try to harm the royal family? She didn't know anyone. She couldn't trust anyone.

She told herself it didn't make any sense to worry. Majid's assassins shot to kill. They hardly anticipated failure. And the royal wing of the hospital was under lockdown. No news would get out. The official story at the palace was that the queen had gone into labor and the king had gone with her. Nobody mentioned Nasir. He always came and went as he pleased. His absence would hardly be noticed.

Still, the news could not be contained forever. People on the street had seen the royal ambulances. The servants at the palace knew what had happened and despite the strictest orders word would get out. What would Majid do then? Send someone to finish the job?

"Dr. Kauffman." Someone called her name as she hurried down the hallway toward Nasir's room.

She turned, surprised by three men in black suits who looked American. "Yes?"

"We've been looking for you," one of them said as they caught up with her. "Agent Maloney," he introduced himself. "The U.S. Embassy in Tihrin was notified that you escaped your kidnappers and were safe at the palace. We're glad to have you back safely. This way." He took her elbow and directed her down the hall.

She looked over the men, trying to figure out who they were. CIA? So they'd been searching for her all this time, and she hadn't been as abandoned as she'd felt. For a moment she wondered who'd called the embassy, then figured it must have been one of Dara's assistants. She was glad Dara remembered to do it. She hadn't. There had been too many things going on.

She followed the men. She could afford a few minutes for explanations. But instead of an empty office, they took her through a side door that lead outside.

"I can't leave," she said, looking at the Lincoln Continental with its black windows.

"Medical personnel at the embassy are waiting to check you over," the agent said. "And we need you to answer some questions before you board the plane home. You'll have a small layover in Germany at one of our military bases, then you're flying straight to Andrew's Airport in D.C."

Home.

She swallowed as the world seemed to stop around her. By tomorrow this time, she could be safe at home. Dara had said there would be fighting soon. The smart thing was definitely to get out while she could. Whatever was going on in Beharrain was none of her business. The members of the royal family were under excellent care. And yet, her steps faltered and she stopped halfway to the car.

"Could you wait a couple of hours?"

The agent's grip tightened on her elbow. "I'm afraid not, Dr. Kauffman. You must understand the situation."

"I do." And because she did, she pulled her arm free. "I'm not going."

The agent glowered at her. "You are in the country of Beharrain illegally. You entered their sovereign territory without a visa."

"I'm here at the invitation and under the protection of Beharrain's king and queen," she said, drawing herself straight, hoping Dara would back her up if asked.

The agents moved closer, an action that felt decidedly threatening.

"You are coming with us," Agent Maloney said, his voice clipped. "You are a U.S. citizen. You cannot get involved in the internal affairs of the Kingdom of Beharrain."

She looked him full in the eye and challenged him. "Are you telling me you're arresting me? On what charges?"

The man took a step back and seemed to try a different approach, speaking this time with a smile on his face. "Of course you're not being arrested, Dr. Kauffman. But you have been through a tremendous ordeal. In your own interest, I strongly urge you to come with us."

"I appreciate your concern, but I am staying. I'll see you at the embassy when I'm done here," she said and turned on her heels, went around the other two agents who stood at her back and marched right into the building again, ignoring when Agent Maloney called after her and implored her to consider her position.

She went through the checkpoint at the door of the royal wing and back to work, sharing her time among the four members of the royal family, doing the best she could, keeping a close eye on anyone who came in touch with them, any treatment they were receiving. As an American doctor and the queen's friend, she was admitted and tolerated everywhere.

By the time Dara was sleeping and her son was content in the arms of one of the nurses, Sadie was about to drop with exhaustion. She checked on the king, out of surgery and weak, but happy at the news of the birth of his son, that his wife was well. Then she moved on to Nasir's room, passing yet another set of guards, and collapsed into the chair next to the bed.

"Are you all right?" he asked, his forehead lined with worry.

"Just tired."

"Why don't you go back to the palace? I will arrange for guards."

"I'm fine here." She just needed to close her eyes for a moment and get her second wind. She'd pulled shifts longer than this when she'd been a resident at St. Agnes Hospital. A few seconds of rest, then she would check on the king and the queen again.

"My brother?"

"He is resting."

"He will pull through?"

"He is getting the best care known to man." She evaded his question. From what the surgeons had told her, the operation was a success, but the injury had been a bad one. Lots of initial blood loss. Despite the best care, there was always the chance of a blood clot or an insidious infection.

Nasir nodded soberly. "And Dara?"

"She's well. She had a boy, did anyone tell you?"

He shook his head as a smile brightened his face. "Another nephew."

"A big boy, healthy," she added. "His name is Aziz."

He reached for her hand and she let him take it, knowing that if any of the doctors came in, he'd be scandalized.

"Thank you for what you've done for me and my family," he said.

"You're welcome."

He held her gaze for a few moments and the strong emotions in his eyes—passion and regret—stole her breath. She looked away.

"You should leave the country," he said, running his thumb over the back of her hand. "There will be unrest."

"So everyone tells me." She took a deep breath and stood up, moved away. "The minister of defense is already taking measures."

An ebony eyebrow slid up his forehead. "Dara?"

"Of course." The queen really was an exceptional woman. She'd been giving advice to the minister over the phone throughout the night.

"You'll leave?" he asked.

"In a few days." She hadn't yet decided exactly.

"I cannot keep you safe." Frustration resonated in his voice.

"Take a break." She smiled. "I will keep *you* safe."

NASIR LEANED onto a windowsill, watching the courtyard below. Other than the stitches that pulled now and then, he felt little of his injury.

He noted the door Ali had gone into, the

window from where the shooter had discharged his weapon. He'd been up in the royal quarters earlier, checking out where Saeed had been shot. The location didn't give him any clues to the shooter's identity.

Something moved below. Sadie. She was walking through the courtyard briskly, coming from the hospital. She spent most of her time there. Saeed was still in critical condition and Dara refused to leave his side. Nasir was allowed to return to the palace, discharged two days after the shooting at his own request. Somebody had to be here.

Sadie looked up and saw him, lifted her arm to wave.

She wore a black burqa, as always, when she left the palace, but her headdress had been pushed back. She usually did that the second she entered the gates.

He watched her golden hair sway with each step as she crossed the courtyard and entered the building. In a few seconds, she was at the door of the throne room where he had been perusing the yard.

"How are they?" he asked as he took in the sight of her. The burqa discarded, she looked splendid in one of the silk creations Dara had gifted her with. This one consisted of loose pants under a kaftanlike top that was a sea of silverish shimmer, the color of the desert moon in winter.

"Saeed is talking more clearly. Dara and Aziz are fine. I think—"

She was interrupted by a knock on the door.

Nasir called out and the guard who entered bowed as he stepped closer.

"Forgive the interruption, Sheik. I have news of Ali ibn Saleh."

"Did you find him?" They'd been looking for the man all morning for questioning. He wanted to know what Ali had been doing in the dark courtyard that night.

"Yes, Sheik," the man said. "He was found buried under some hay in one of the stables. He'd been stabbed to death."

Nasir pushed away from the window. "Have the stables been secured?"

"The security chief is there. They are brushing for fingerprints and checking security cameras."

There would be sufficient footage, at least.

The stables were one of the most highly secured areas of the royal palace aside from the royal quarters. Saeed owned a number of Arabian stallions that were worth millions. The Englishman who'd been brought in to set up the stables years ago had taken his job seriously.

"Has anyone called the police?"

"No."

"Good. I don't want news of this beyond the palace. Our security will handle it." Any trouble, any sign of weakness within the palace would play into Majid's hands. He dismissed the guard, waited until he left before turning to Sadie and telling her what had happened. "I want to arrange for the king's private plane to take you to safety."

SADIE CONSIDERED his offer, but didn't feel any more ready to leave than she had two days ago when the CIA had come for her. "In a few days. No assassin will be gunning for me. I'm nobody important here."

"There is such thing as being in the wrong place at the wrong time." Nasir's face was closed, his thoughts impossible to guess.

The paleness had vanished from his skin and he seemed to have recovered fully, although she thought he was taking on too much work too fast, spending nearly every minute of his day investigating the assassination attemps.

"The children are here, Salah and the girls," she pointed out.

Although Dara was cleared to leave the hospital, she had chosen to stay near Saeed, keeping little Aziz with her as well. The older children were in the care of their nannies, talking to their mother over the phone several times a day, sending cute messages with Sadie each time she went in to check on the king and the queen.

"Where the princes and princesses go is the king's and queen's decision," Nasir said. "Dara won't leave Saeed. And Saeed won't send her away against her will. He sent Salah and our sisters away during the upheaval when Majid was removed from the throne. It backfired. We nearly lost them."

"If the children are safe here then so am I."

"It's different." He held her gaze.

"Why?"

"It's not your fight. You need not risk anything."

"I won't. I'll go in a few days."

He did not try to dissuade her further, but acknowledged her decision with a nod. "I must go to the stables. Let me call a guard to escort you back to your room."

"I'll go with you." That way when Dara asked her later she would be able to give a full report.

"It might be..." Nasir hesitated. "You should rest. When was the last time you slept?" His gaze was soft with concern.

"I'm a doctor. I'm used to this."

He nodded before he turned. She fell in step next to him.

"You think Ali was one of the spies?" she asked.

"It's possible. Or he could have seen something he wasn't supposed to."

True. He could have been sneaking around stealing or meeting a woman. He might have bumped into someone else in the night, someone who was doing something more sinister. But then, why not kill Ali on the spot? Unless Ali remained unseen and later tried to blackmail the man. He could have gotten killed because of that.

Of course, all of that was pure speculation.

They knew only one thing for sure. There was a murderer in the palace.

Chapter Eight

Sadie had not visited the stables before and now regretted the oversight. The building itself was a work of art, the horses the most sublime creatures she had ever encountered. She followed Nasir's gaze to above the door where a smashed security camera hung from a wire. Then Nasir moved forward and she followed.

Based on the building's sheer size, she'd expected heat and the strong smell of manure, but the stalls were almost impossibly clean and orderly, the smell of horses and hay welcoming. And after a moment, she realized that the faint whirring sound coming from above was the climate control.

"Amazing," she said, and glanced into a tack room that practically gleamed.

Nasir smiled at her reaction. "You have to understand, among our people, and especially in my family, horses are nearly a religion."

"And yet, you ride a camel," she observed.

"Ronu is my friend," he said.

"Where is he now?"

"Home. He's been returned to my tribe. That's the place he likes the best."

Like his owner, she thought. Her gaze was drawn to the lacquered wood stall doors that displayed brass plaques with flowing Arabic script on each, probably the names of the horses. Equipment and tools hung from pegs, the place nearly as ordered as an operating room. She would have gladly seen more, but the moment was not appropriate for gawking. They were at a murder scene. The back of the stables was crowded with security personnel.

Horses snorted as they passed by, slammed their feet to the ground, whinnied, probably disturbed by the number of people and the palpable tension in the air.

The security guards fell silent as Nasir and she reached them. Two of the men stepped aside, giving her a glimpse of what they'd been looking at.

The body lay amid scattered hay, the blood on the man's clothes already dried, his face ashen. He'd been dead for several hours.

The sight of death didn't bother her. In her work, she'd seen it enough, even violent death—stab and gunshot wounds were common in the emergency room. But there was always a pang of regret that came with cases like this. The man had been neither old nor diseased, his death senseless and unnecessary, not caused by an unstoppable force like cancer, but by the whim of another man.

Nasir was asking the guards questions as he stepped forward and walked around the victim in a wide circle, to avoid contaminating evidence she supposed.

She looked at the victim's injuries, wishing she understood Arabic so she would know what Nasir was saying. She'd picked up a few words: thank you, hello and good-bye, yes and no. She knew that *souk* meant market, *khubz* was bread and *khanjar* the Bedu's curved dagger. She tried to pick out something from the rapidly spoken exchange next to her now, but was distracted when another uniformed man joined them, a large plastic case in hand. He greeted Nasir and the others, set his case down and opened it.

"I don't want to involve anyone from outside of the palace," Nasir said to her. "Tariq is the forensics expert on the security team. He was off site today because his mother is ill. It took the security chief a while to find him."

That palace security had a forensics expert surprised her, although after a moment of thinking she realized it shouldn't have. The royal palace didn't lack modern technology. But in many ways the culture was so traditional that the contrast between the old customs and new gadgets was sometimes startling.

Tariq, a slim man about the same height she was, said something in Arabic, and the men around the body all took two steps back. He pulled a camera from his case and started snapping pictures.

"Who will do the autopsy?" she asked Nasir.

"There won't be one. Islam considers it the desecration of the human body."

And there it was again. The old, side by side with the new. Forensics yes, autopsy no. "An autopsy might give clues to who the murderer is," she argued.

Nasir shook his head. "And you can't examine Ali, either."

Probably because she was a woman. Not that she'd thought to ask to be allowed to take a closer look. She wasn't a coroner. But now that Nasir brought the issue up... She *was* a doctor. She moved so she would have an unobstructed view and began to catalog the man's injuries.

Multiple incised wounds crisscrossed the scalp, face and neck. She also spotted defense wounds on both hands. Ali had fought for his life, and since most of his wounds were nonfatal sharp force injuries, it looked like he'd fought off his attacker for a fair length of time.

"Anything you want to share?" Nasir asked on a low voice next to her.

She glanced at him and found him watching her with some amusement. He'd guessed what she was doing.

She told him about the defense wounds,

keeping her voice low, barely above a whisper, not wanting to draw the attention of the security team who were helping the forensic expert now. She never knew who around her spoke English, who would disapprove what she was doing. Her goal was to help Nasir, not to cause further trouble by offending local custom.

She focused on the body. "Sharp force wound on the neck, right side, with transaction of right internal jugular vein." She judged the wound path to be about four inches. "The injury is rostal," she said, then added, "upward," when Nasir drew up an eyebrow.

"Does that mean the killer was a shorter man?" he asked.

"Not necessarily. Could be that's just how he was holding the weapon when he finally got through Ali's blocking."

He nodded.

She was already looking at the vertically oriented stab wound on the right side of the chest. Since Ali's blood-soaked shirt covered much of the wound, she could not make a guess to its size. She figured the location around the seventh rib. Judging from the amount of blood, the knife, or whatever other sharp weapon the killer had used, had entered the right pleural cavity. "I can't say for sure without an autopsy, but my best guess is that his right lung was also ruptured and hemorrhaged," she said. "Another fatal wound."

"So our killer was a thorough man. Anything else?"

She looked over the man one more time. "That's as much as I can tell standing this far and him fully dressed. He has lacerations all over, but all minor. I would say whoever the killer was, they were closely matched in strength. The knife made the difference."

The forensic expert turned the body to its side, and she moved a little forward to be able to see the back. No apparent injuries there, although there was blood on the man's shirt on his right side. She figured it had come from the side stab wound.

"Looks like he was attacked head-on. The knife had been out from the get go." She'd seen no sign of blunt force injury to the face, no indication that there was a hustle, that punches flew then the knife was pulled in the heat of the fight.

The attacker, whoever he was, had come to Ali with the intent to kill.

SHE COULDN'T SLEEP. Sadie slipped from her bed and walked to the table to pour a glass of water. She'd seen death and plenty of it, yet the picture of Ali as he'd lain in the hay would not let her rest.

Her brain was crowded with questions. Who killed the man? Why? What on earth was she still doing here instead of hightailing it to home and safety?

She needed a short walk to tire her body out enough to sleep. She changed into one of the outfits she'd received from Dara—a pair of simple pants in pale blue silk with a matching long tunic. All she planned on doing was to walk around the hallways of the queen's quarters, admire the artwork, let it calm her. But once she was out of her room, she thought of the garden and the fresh air up there, the beauty of the starlit sky.

What was the best way to get there from here? *The hallway with the botanical marble carvings.* She padded down the corridor, not bothering to turn up the lights that were set on low.

Two guards snapped to attention in front of the doors to the queen's quarters as soon as she peeked out. She simply nodded to them and went on. One of them followed. *So much for solitude.* But the man did not truly bother her, keeping a good distance. With a murderer on the loose, she was actually comforted by his presence, although she didn't think she was a target.

Three men had been picked so far. Saeed and Nasir were logical choices—the king and his brother. Majid would want them out of the way. And Ali had been involved in all of that somehow. Nasir and she had seen him from the roof as he was sneaking around in the middle of the night.

She reached the top of the staircase and stepped into the garden, transported instantly by the landscape that seemed otherworldly in the moonlight. She cast off her slippers, choosing the grass instead of the brick pathway, enjoying the slight dew that cooled her feet.

She lost herself among the palm trees and soon found herself alone. Good. The guard was smart enough to figure out she needed privacy, and respectful enough to give it to her. She was certain he was still there, just outside of her line of vision.

She meandered around for a while before she came to the low wall that edged the garden, the same spot from where she'd first seen Ali before. Where had he gone then? Whom had he met?

His murderer?

She shivered and glanced around. Wouldn't have minded having that guard within sight now. Then she heard the sound of feet on gravel and relaxed. The man was still here.

The footsteps died. She glanced back in time to see a shadow separate from the trees. Her heart sped as she recognized the man walking toward her.

"Are you all right?" Nasir's voice was laced with concern.

His solid presence brought a wave of

comfort. She took in his mussed black hair and his clothes: a pair of dark slacks and a white shirt, the buttons hastily done.

"I couldn't sleep," she said. "What are you doing here?"

"Security called me." He smiled, looking more relaxed now, his white teeth a contrast to his olive skin in the dark. "They weren't sure what to do about you."

He came closer and leaned to the half wall next to her, looked down.

That special awareness she felt every time he was near zinged to life.

She tried to think of something intelligent to say, something that wouldn't betray how much his nearness affected her. "How is your injury? Any redness around the wounds?"

He shrugged it off. "It's fine."

He'd been working way too much when he should have been resting. Even now, he was here in the middle of the night, instead of sleeping in bed—which was her fault.

"I didn't realize— I'm sorry the guards woke you."

He turned his attention from the courtyard to her. "I'm not." His gaze was intent on her face, as if trying to read her mind.

She hoped he couldn't. It was full of observations on how handsome he looked in the moonlight, the tempting line of his mouth, his mesmerizing eyes, his wide chest.

"I've never met anyone like you," he said, and although his eyes smiled, he sounded exasperated.

She gave a small, nervous laugh. "Ditto."

He looked back at the courtyard below. "I'm not sure what to do."

"You'll have the forensic report by morning. You increased security already," she said, then from the way he glanced back at her, she realized she had misunderstood him. He wasn't sure what to do about *her.*

Was he leaning closer? Hard to tell with bushes swaying in the background. The moonlight was deceiving.

"Dr. Sadie Kauffman." He said her name full of formality, as if to remind himself who she was. "It is not good for you to share my company. My life is too dangerous."

"So is mine," she shot back. They had

met at a bandit camp. She'd been up to her neck in danger when he rode in.

"I would do anything to see you safe."

She wouldn't have wanted to be anywhere else right then. "I feel safe," she said, and added silently, *when I'm with you.*

"You do not recognize danger," he responded.

Then all of a sudden he was close enough for their lips to touch.

The kiss was neither sweet nor gentle, perhaps to show her just how much jeopardy she was in. He didn't explore her mouth; he conquered it.

But in every small movement, in every sound that escaped his throat was his blinding, barely restrained need for her. And it reached her as nothing else could, awakened a responding need deep inside.

Madness, she thought, but thinking no longer figured into the equation between them.

By the time he pulled back, abruptly, her heart was going a million beats per minute, her lungs gasping for air.

"I apolog—"

"Don't." She pressed her lips against his.

"Sadie," he whispered, and his arms came around her body with infinite tenderness. He traced her mouth with his. "What are we to do?"

"We'll deal with it," she said between two kisses.

He gave a strangled laugh. "You are a most practical woman."

She wanted to remark on that, but his hands slid to her sides then up on her rib cage, building a blockade of sensation between her brain and her mouth.

She reached up to steady herself, and her palms stayed pressed to his chest. She was floating in pleasure.

No, she really was floating—in his arms. He had picked her up without letting their lips separate. Where was he taking her? Did she care?

They didn't go far, just to a spot where the palm trees above touched together, keeping the grass dry beneath them. Here he laid her down, away from prying eyes that could have seen them from the courtyard or any of a number of windows that looked toward the garden wall where they'd stood before.

She kept her arms around him, pulled his head back to hers as soon as she was on solid ground.

"Poems should be written about your beauty," he said when they broke for air.

The odd expression on his face gave her pause. "Is something wrong?"

"I'm a terrible poet. All Bedu are supposed to be good at this. It's our national pastime."

She wouldn't have guessed *that.* The Bedu she'd seen, with their rifles slung over their shoulders and daggers stuck in their belts, looked more like warriors than poets. But just like the land they lived on, they were a complex people with many sides, and much hidden beauty.

"It's okay," she reassured him. "I was never into poetry. Too much symbolism confuses me. I'm more of a *just the facts* person. Science major."

He gave her a half smile, then his handsome face turned serious. "The fact is, I'm falling for a woman I can never have."

Time seemed to stop around them, as if even the night was holding its breath.

His words sobered her. He could have had her, in fact, whether he knew it or not. Right then and there. She wanted it, ached for him. But she realized now as she looked into the intense fire in his eyes, that they would not go any further, not tonight, perhaps not ever. He had too much honor for that.

The primary feeling was disappointment, then came appreciation for the kind of man he was. How many times, when she was being backstabbed over promotions in the hospital, had she lamented that there were no more men who lived by principles, none who would sacrifice temporary gain for fairness or justice or faith or whatever value he held important and believed. Well, here was one in front of her now.

She watched him as he rolled onto his back and stared at the silhouette of palm fronds above them. After a moment, she curled against his side, her head resting on his chest.

Odd how much intimacy could be in something as innocent as that, just the two of them lying side by side, barely touching. Yet for the moment, they were one.

"So, I suppose, you're promised to the daughter of another sheik," she said jokingly, trying to lighten the mood between them, trying to pretend she wasn't fighting herself to beg him to make love to her.

He took a deep breath. "As I understand, Saeed has been negotiating."

His words were as shocking as a bucket of ice water would have been just then.

She sat up, confused and angered. "Oh, my God." She could barely squeeze the words through her constricting throat as pain and betrayal squeezed her chest. "Care to tell me what in hell we were doing here then?"

She scrambled to stand, but he reached for her, came to his knees to pull her back down until they were kneeling face-to-face, her hands restrained in his. "It's not like that. I don't even know if a specific woman has been discussed yet. It's tradition."

Bitterness gathered in her throat as she looked away, only half hearing his words. "When are you going to marry her?" she asked even as she knew that she had no reason to be this hurt, this angry. What claim did she have on the man? What had he promised her? What had they had between them? Two kisses. In her world that would have been nothing. But they were in his world now. And in her heart… God, she was stupid.

She had come to care more for Nasir than for any other man she'd ever dated. More than she'd cared for Brian, the man she had almost married—would have married if he hadn't dumped her the second she was no longer necessary for the advancement of his career.

"I cannot marry of my brother's choosing." His voice was quiet but strong. "I see that now."

She breathed a lungful of air. Why did those words feel so wonderful? What did it all matter? She was still planning on going back to the U.S. in a couple of days.

The night surrounded them with perfect silence, the garden with surreal beauty. She grasped for something that was real. What she was beginning to feel for Nasir couldn't be. She barely knew him. He was from a different world. He had duties and obligations to his title, to his tribe. They had separate lives that could never fit together.

"I'll be going back to the U.S.," she said, as much to Nasir as to herself. She needed to hear it, needed the stability of having a plan. "I'd like to come back someday," she added, because the thought of never returning was too painful. "I'd like to go out to the desert, make some notes on tribal medicine."

"There's someone I know who can tell you all about that. When you come back, I'll take you to her." He stood with the lithe grace of a warrior, helped her up, but let go of her hands immediately after.

His face was closed, his gaze unfathomable.

The swift shock of disappointment surprised her. What had she expected? That he would beg her to stay?

The chirp of Nasir's cell phone broke the silence between them. He looked at the number and answered in Arabic, his face growing darker and darker as he listened.

"What happened?" she asked when he closed the phone and slid it back into his pocket.

"The night guard found another body."

Chapter Nine

Nasir's blood heated with anger as he took in the crime scene, feeling shocked and saddened. Wahab, one of the secretaries, hung limp from a rope attached to the scaffolding behind the administrative offices, his eyes bulging, the tips of his fingers bloodied. He had clawed them raw, trying to get the rope off.

"No attempt to hide the body this time," the head of security said next to him.

"No, but it's the middle of the night. Whoever killed him might have figured nobody would come this way until morning."

He nodded to the men to cut Wahab down and glanced at Sadie, who stood to the left of him. "Do you see anything that can help us?" he asked, realizing he was growing too used to having her at his side, being able to count on her opinion, on her help.

In cities like Tihrin, the women led separate lives in their own part of the house. But the Bedu, whose ways he preferred, had more of a partnership between husband and wife. Nomadic life was difficult, relying on each other a necessity. And he could all too easily imagine Sadie at his side, healing his people, adding her opinion to his, curled against him at night.

He shut down that train of thought and switched his focus back to the body on the ground as he waited for her response.

"Blunt force trauma to the back of the head," she said. "Someone knocked him out before stringing him up, but he revived at one point. He was fully conscious while he slowly suffocated. He fought it."

"Can you tell when he was killed?"

"Not more than three or four hours ago. No sign of rigor mortis yet."

He nodded and spoke to the guards, giving orders for notifying Wahab's family and releasing the unfortunate man's body to them.

"Come," he said to Sadie. He wanted to be alone with her, to be able to talk unguarded, which was not an easy task since he could not take her to his room or go with her into the queen's quarters.

"We'll go back to the garden," he said after a moment. The garden was open to everyone who lived and worked at the palace and therefore considered one of its "public" places, where men and women could be present at the same time without having to worry about offending anyone's honor.

He led the way to the east wing and up the stairs. Sadie walked quietly beside him, lost in her own thoughts. He didn't stop until he reached the half wall that overlooked the courtyard.

"I never asked what the forensic report found on Ali," she said behind him.

"Not much." He turned. "No fingerprints in the stables that didn't belong to people who work there. Which could mean the killer was one of them, or that he wore gloves, or that he didn't touch anything save the knife he used to kill Ali."

"Has that been found?"

He shook his head.

"An autopsy could have given us a lot more information on the weapon. We could have found out if it was a straight knife or a curved dagger, how long it was."

"Ali's family would never agree. He'll be buried before the day is out."

"So soon?"

"Muslim burials happen within twenty-four hours of death."

"In some countries, when crimes are involved, the district attorney's office can request exhumation of the body," she remarked.

He found the very thought offensive and distasteful. "In some countries, they respect the human body and consider death Allah's will."

She didn't argue with him, but stepped up to the wall next to him and looked down.

"Do you think the same man killed both Ali and Wahab?" he asked, aware in the back of his head how unusual a conversation this was. Any conversation with her was out of the norm, really. Single men did not get many opportunities to chat with single women. Even with his own wife, a man who lived in the city might only meet at meal-times and at night in the bedroom, their conversations limited to the children and household matters. The Bedu saw each other more during the day, and Bedu women enjoyed more freedom, but still, could it ever be enough for a Western woman?

He thought of Saeed and Dara's thoroughly modern marriage. If they could make it work, then why couldn't he and Sadie? Because Sadie was leaving, he reminded himself. The thought left him in a dark mood as he perused the courtyard below.

"They could have been both killed by the same man," she said slowly, seeming to consider the question with care. "The killer might have used whatever opportunity he came across. He had a knife handy when he got Ali alone. And out back behind the offices, there were scaffolding and rope."

Nasir stared in front of him. How many spies did Majid have in the palace? One? Two? More? Were Ali and Wahab among them? "Why were these two killed?" He voiced the question on his mind.

"They weren't key people," Sadie said. "I mean, it's not as if they had to be out of the way so Majid could come back. Not like you and the king."

He nodded.

"So they were either Majid's spies and someone thought they'd been compromised, or they knew who Majid's spies were and were killed before they could share their knowledge with palace security."

They'd been coming up with bits and pieces of a theory over the last few days, but the way Sadie put the possibility into words was the most clearly defined yet.

"Let's say that Ali was one of Majid's men," he thought out loud. "How did anyone know that we saw him from the roof and suspected him?"

"Did you tell anyone?"

"I gave an order to security to have him followed."

"You trust every man in palace security?"

He didn't have to think about that. "They are all men of our tribe. They would all give their lives for Saeed and our family."

"If—" She started to say something, then paused. "Okay, so back to Ali. Did security find out what he was doing behind that door?"

"By the time they got there he was gone. There's nothing there but offices. He could have gone for something as innocent as borrowing pen and paper. Or he could have gone to meet a friend."

"He didn't look innocent," she said.

He had to agree with her. The man had kept looking around as he hurried across the courtyard, as if he was afraid of someone seeing him.

But they *had* seen him, he and Sadie, although he didn't think Ali had spotted them on the roof. But what if someone else had? "What if someone saw us up here as we watched Ali?"

Sadie's eyes widened as she turned toward the courtyard and scanned the wall on the other side. "Ten windows."

He pulled the phone from his pocket and

called security, ordered all the rooms searched and requested an exhaustive list of who had access to each.

"So whoever Ali was visiting could have been watching for him from one of the windows," he said after he put the phone away.

"Right. And he saw us spot Ali. He figured sooner or later Ali would be questioned."

"I was waiting on that to see if he would lead us to his accomplices first. I didn't want him to know that we suspected him."

"And the night you were shot at, the shadow I saw was in one of those windows, too," she said.

She'd told him about that before, but now it suddenly gained new meaning. Previously he had thought that the killer had the assassination attempts all planned out and was following him when he was shot at. But what if, as in the murder of Ali and Wahab, the killer was also opportunistic in his attempts to shoot Nasir and Saeed? He could have seen Nasir in the courtyard by chance, took a shot at him, then figured he would use the ensuing chaos among security to go after the king.

"It seems our killer spent a lot of time behind those windows. He was there to see us up here watching Ali. And he was there again just as I came into the courtyard." He'd hid behind the bushes because he heard someone coming after him, footsteps that turned out to be Sadie's.

"You think he might live behind one of those windows?"

"He either lives or works there." The window Sadie had identified opened off a corridor. The killer could have been walking through there on his way to or from his room or office.

He looked at the ten windows he had picked out for security. The lights were on behind all ten. They were being searched.

His phone chirped. The display showed the call was coming from the head of security.

"We found a bloody towel in Abbas's desk," the man said.

Abbas. The betrayal was like a blade slicing his flesh. So Abbas was keeping his two wives on Majid's money. "Bring him to security for questioning."

"We cannot find him, Sheik. He's not in the palace."

WHEN SADIE WALKED into the dining room for breakfast, Nasir was already there. Since they'd arrived at the palace he'd been wearing suits, but this morning he wore the traditional dress of his people—not in ragged clothes like he'd worn at the bandit camp, but in a stunning white robe fit for a sheik. The fine material accentuated his wide shoulders as he read through some papers, the remnants of his breakfast on the plate in front of him.

His dark hair was combed neatly into place, but his eyes were shadowed. He didn't look like he'd slept any more than she had.

He looked up as a servant pulled a chair out for her, at a respectable distance from him. The servant would stay for the whole duration of breakfast. It had been like that since Saeed and Dara had been in the hospital.

She didn't mind the extra person in the room. He helped dispel the intimacy of shared meals, helped to remind her not to wish for things she couldn't have.

"Good morning." Nasir's voice reached across the table and touched her.

His dark gaze focused on her face. Even tired after a night of chasing a killer, he was the most handsome man she'd ever met, and the most powerful.

Last night, he'd insisted that she go to sleep, and at two in the morning she'd agreed. He'd wanted to join the security force in searching for Abbas, and she understood that she couldn't help him with that. She would only be in the way. The men on the security force felt uncomfortable around her—they weren't used to working with a woman.

"You slept well?" he asked as he dipped a small, round spoon into a crystal container of honey and let the thick-spun gold drip into his tea.

The honey reminded her of Mussafa's pleasure palace, which brought to mind their kiss from the night before, and the dreams from which she'd recently awakened. Desire sang inside her—sharp, powerful chords resonating through her body.

She nodded and looked down to her plate, filling it from the platters in front of her with olives and white cheese, a slice of Arabic bread. "Yes, thank you," she said. "Have you found Abbas?"

She found his gaze still on her when she looked up.

"No," he said. "He left both of his houses." He paused for a moment. "It's beginning."

Her hand stopped halfway to her mouth. She set down the piece of cheese she was about to taste. "The fighting?"

He nodded somberly. "Rumors are circulating among the tribes that Saeed and I are dead."

"But you've been on television." Nasir had briefly appeared at a news conference after he'd gotten out of the hospital to make sure the nation was reassured. He had admitted the king had been injured, but he'd downplayed the injury and spun the news in a positive direction by announcing that a new male heir had been born.

"Lots of people don't have access to television," he was saying now. "Not the nomadic tribes. Majid has been poisoning them against the king. It will be days before the truth reaches them." He took a sip of his tea then set the cup down. "Saeed and Dara are coming home today, and little Aziz."

"Saeed?" She looked at him confused. It was way too soon.

"Against doctors' recommendations," Nasir said. "He wants to be back in the palace and wants the people to know it. The palace doctors will be treating him."

She supposed it would be sufficient. The king's own doctors and nurses could probably provide him with the same level of care as the hospital now that he was out of intensive care.

"You should leave," he said as he watched her.

"I feel safe in the palace."

"I'm returning to the desert. I was just waiting for you so I could tell you. I must talk to the sheiks, must let them see me alive, tell them that the king is yet living, make them see the evil that Majid is planning. He is recruiting heavily from the southern tribes. The people are confused. If they think Saeed is dead, they might think they have no other choice but to join Majid and support him in returning to Tihrin to take the throne."

"I want to go with you," she said then fell silent, surprised by the words that came out of her mouth without conscious thought.

Nasir shook his head with force. "It is unsafe in the desert right now.

"Not if I'm with you."

"Especially if you're with me." His dark gaze held her bound.

THE BRAND-NEW military jeep Saeed had given him had its advantages, Nasir had to admit. Comfort, for one, and speed. He watched the sand as he drove in a wide circle around the camp of his own *fakhadh* to see if he could find any unfamiliar tracks that shouldn't have been there, signs that would tell him whether Majid's men had come this far already and were watching the camp. He had made the full circle without spotting anything worthy of notice, so he turned the jeep toward the tents.

He glanced over to Sadie and found her watching him with an amused grin over her face.

"You just love flying over the sand, don't you?" she asked.

"I love the desert." The vast open land seemed to have no end. The sense of freedom and history were like the blood flowing in his veins. He couldn't have lived without it. Not that he expected anyone but the dwindling Bedu to understand him.

The new generations of Beharrainians lived and worked in the villages and towns. The rich organized desert hunts now and then. Even those who worked in the desert on the oil wells tended to live in town and commute. For most of his people, the desert was something to visit. It had ceased to be their home.

"You belong here," she said matter-of-factly.

He nodded, not entirely surprised that she would understand—she was a most astute woman. And he was glad that she had come, although he'd strongly advised her not to.

But Dara had walked in on the argument, home from the hospital, listened for a few minutes then given them an odd look. She defied his expectations when rather than insisting on keeping her new American friend safe at the palace, the queen had said that she thought Sadie *should* go, if that was what she wanted.

He hadn't had the time to stay and fight the both of them, as stubborn as they were. He couldn't convince them to do what was safest and most reasonable. And he wouldn't have been arguing with his full heart anyhow. He wanted Sadie with him, to enjoy her company for as long as possible, and to be able to defend her if she met with danger. He'd been reluctant to leave her in the care of the palace guards, as excellent as they were. And so, in the end, he had agreed.

She should be safe by his side while visiting the rest of the tribes. They had already stopped by two camps on the way to his. People were unsettled, but his presence and the message he carried from their king seemed to soothe their anxieties. The two camps he and Sadie had already visited pledged their allegiance anew to the rightful king.

Sadie was treated with all the respect befitting a friend of the queen who traveled under a sheik's protection. She had treated the sick and earned each camp's admiration by the time they left.

She was the most amazing woman he had ever met. Nasir stole another glance at her then waved to the sentries he'd set and drove past them into camp. He parked next to the beat-up pickups the men used to get to town to sell their goods at the market.

His cell phone rang just as he got out of the car. He listened to new information from one of Saeed's men and thanked him for the news before hanging up.

"What is it?" Sadie was watching him.

"Majid has been successful in recruiting farther south. His band now has a couple of thousand men. The royal army was sent out to meet them, but they refused to surrender."

"How far from here?"

"Less than a hundred kilometers," he said and scanned the men in camp, estimating how many he could take with him to join the fight, how many he should leave here with the women and children. They weren't in any danger yet, but once Majid's troops disbanded and scattered, who knew which way they would go.

"I need to talk to the men," he said.

She nodded and went to join the women.

Nasir let his gaze linger over her, over the children who ran up to her and surrounded her like bees to the hive. She'd won over his *fakhadh* as she had the other two camps. She was ready to care for the sick, help the women with their chores, to eat the food no matter what local "delicacy" was put in front of her. She was discovering Bedu life with unbridled enthusiasm.

He had to leave soon, stand in for Saeed in the fight. The army had to see one of them. He knew that and wanted to face Majid, but at the same time, he hated to leave his people. He hated to leave Sadie.

She joined the women over the cooking fire and was now looking through a rolled up rag that was carefully lined with herbs, her whole being focused on what Shadia was saying next to her.

Shadia, an old servant woman well-versed in medicine who'd been with Nasir's family since before his father's time, kept an eye on everything that went on in the camp around them. Her glance glided over Nasir and paused a moment before it moved on smoothly. He turned away. By Allah, he had it bad. He hadn't spent this much time staring at the women's section since his adolescent years.

He walked toward his tent and called out to a handful of men who were cleaning sheepskin in the shade of another tent. They rose to join him, passed the word along to others. In a few minutes, nearly every man in camp was crowded into his tent. After two hours of talking and drinking spiced coffee, they came to an agreement on who would stay to protect the women and children and who would go with him into the fight.

He would have preferred more to stay, but felt fortunate to have talked as many into it as he had. All wanted the glory of battle.

Among the Bedu the sheik did not rule as a dictator. Decisions were arrived at based on consensus of the elders of the tribe, although the sheik's opinion was carefully weighed.

The men left to prepare, while he remained in his tent to once again go over the hastily prepared maps, drawings they'd made of the area where the fight would take place, how the dunes had been the last time the herd was taken that way. It wasn't much. A lot could have changed since then—the landscape of the desert could change in a single day from a single sandstorm—but it was better than nothing.

He looked up at the soft sound of leather sandals on sand and something caught in his chest. The sight of Sadie, wearing the traditional clothes of his people, bringing him food. Behind her, the tents that had meant home to him painted a picture that brought to life dreams he had not dared to acknowledge.

For this moment she belonged here, was part of his life. And with a ferocious, sudden need, he wanted it to stay that way forever.

"I'm not sure what this is," she said with

a smile as she set down the tray, "but Shadia says you like it."

"Roast mutton with spicy rice." The dish was his favorite.

"She knows amazing things. Her cures are beautifully simple. Half the time I think, no way is that going to work. But then they do. She has an amazing grasp of the human body and how it's connected to its environment. She should have a doctorate in holistic healing."

"She has the love and respect of her people. Either she or her mother birthed nearly every person in this camp. She has saved everybody's life at least once, including mine."

"It boggles the mind to know people like that. To know a patient all his life, from birth, to be able to observe daily habits, to know his medical heritage by closely knowing the parents and grandparents. It's not that I don't have access to information back at the hospital. I can get tests run and labwork and whatever. But Shadia heals without any of that. She has knowledge I envy."

He smiled at the fervent way she said those words. "You must remember, modern medical science is only a few hundred years old. Our tribal medicine is a few thousand years old."

She smiled back. "Right there, that thought, it blows me away. It's—" She hesitated.

"What is it?"

"It's been a while since medicine has been this exciting for me." She looked to Shadia then back at him. "People on TV are always saying how the rain forests are disappearing and hundreds of plants become extinct every year that could cure diseases, and tribal medicine gets lost, and now here I am at a place where it still exists. This is it." She was grinning with enthusiasm. "This is it," she emphasized.

A couple of men walked by, each with several rifles swung over their backs.

"Where are they going?" She turned after them.

"To war," he said, hating to ruin her good mood. "I'm taking a small group with me tonight."

She fell silent and still, watching him for a while before she said, "Be careful."

"You, too." He would not take his eyes off her, wanting to memorize the way she looked at this moment, take that into the fight with him. "You'll be safe here." He prayed to Allah that it'd be so, offered his life for hers if a life must be taken.

His thoughts were underscored by gunfire in the distance.

Chapter Ten

Sadie turned in time to see a speeding blue pickup come right up to the barbed wire that kept the camels from entering the camp. A handful of Nasir's men jumped off the back and ran to him.

She moved out of the way, wishing she could understand what they were saying. She caught only one word: Majid. Between that and the frantic pointing to the south, the situation wasn't too hard to figure out. Majid was coming. And if he was coming, he wasn't coming alone.

She took off running toward Nasir's tent to find Shadia. Majid was bringing the fight to them. They better get ready to treat the injured.

EVERY VEHICLE at camp was circled around the handful of tents that sheltered the women and children. The men who'd brought the news that Majid was coming said he was just a few miles away.

Calls had been made to the rest of the tribe, but the other camps were too far. The enemy would be here in minutes.

"Collapse all the tents outside the blockade," Nasir shouted over the clamor and rushed to help. "Make it look like they caught us in the middle of taking down the camp."

He grabbed a tent pole and heaved it out of the sand, let it fall to the carpets. He climbed from the collapsed tent and went to the next, asking the women to help by scattering things outside. They had to make Majid believe that they'd been about to run away, that maybe some of them were gone already. "Let's get as many fighters under these as we can. Lie flat," he told the men nearest to him and they passed on his words.

He looked around and saw no panic, only his orders carried out with speed. This was his family, his *fakhadh*. They trusted his judgment and had been working together all their lives. And right now Sadie, too, was part of the ordered chaos, part of his people, doing her share. There were no individuals, only one people with one goal and fierce courage. Pride swelled in him, but with it fear. He was the sheik—each life his responsibility.

He saw to it that as many men as possible were hidden under the collapsed tents without making their presence obvious, then withdrew the rest behind the blockade. He chose a spot that faced the attack coming from the south, and asked the men to shift the cars to create a small gap, an obvious "weakness" in the blockade that would draw the attackers. At the last minute, he drove the water truck inside the blockade and parked it to shield the tents that protected the women and children at the center.

The enemy came in a cloud of dust, in pickups. Majid had left his military trucks behind. The ploy had worked. The air force had mistaken his band of a hundred or so bandits for a group of tribal warriors and had not taken them out from the air.

Nasir waited, holding his men, as the enemy began shooting long before they were in range. He stood behind the barricade on a stack of crates, tall and visible. He wanted Majid to see him, to come to him, to focus on him alone, be too distracted to pay attention to the collapsed tents that littered the sand on each side.

For a while the plan worked, and he felt a moment of hope, despite the fact that they were obviously outgunned. Majid had used the money he had secreted away to banks in foreign countries while he'd been on the throne to equip himself with the latest technology available on the black market. Weapons dealers were his main supporters, so his men were equipped as well as any special forces units.

The enemy had weapons with longer range than Nasir's men. He waited, held the line even as men around him fell. Then they were close enough, and he gave the signal. The first gunshots went off almost simultaneously, filling the air with thunder.

Responding bullets slammed into the circled vehicles, few finding their true aim.

Nasir was aware of every one of his men who fell, of every bullet that slammed into the water truck that now leaked, but was blocking the tents and keeping them safe. The women and children in those tents were the future of his tribe. And Sadie—

He aimed his rifle and took out the driver of the closest pickup.

Two other enemy vehicles had already been disabled, several of the enemy injured, the rest returning fire. Majid still led the line, riding for the weak spot in the blockade, riding for Nasir. Then they were close enough, in the open wedge of the collapsed tents.

At that moment, Nasir shouted the battle cry of the Bedu, his people joining in, their voices rising above the sounds of gunfire. The men hidden in the tents sprang up and attacked the enemy. At the same time, Nasir and the men remaining with him came outside of the barricade.

The enemy was surrounded on three sides and realized it now, the drivers slamming on their brakes, trying to turn around, two of the pickups smashing into each other, one overturning. Some tried to run over Nasir's men, who were out in the open, so for the next several minutes their main goal became disabling the vehicles, hitting the tires, the radiators, shattering windshields, taking out the drivers.

"I'm Bedu!" Some of his men shouted the ancient war cry to gain strength from that, reminding each other of their ancestors and the battles they'd fought before.

"Allah be gloried!" others shouted on each side.

Men were fighting hand-to-hand now, with guns, knives and bare knuckles. He shoved off the body of a bandit who had jumped on him from the back of a pickup, then saw from the corner of his eye as one of his men, Abu, fought three who surrounded him. Nasir aimed and picked off two, helping the man out. Abu, the father of nine sons who'd all gone the day before to join the king's army, took care of his remaining opponent quickly now that his attention was no longer divided.

"I was just playing with them, Sheik." The old man grinned at him, and nodded his thanks as he threw himself into the thick of the battle again.

Nasir ducked the butt of a rifle that was coming toward his head from the left and lunged at his attacker. *Abbas*. The traitor at the palace; he recognized the man. Their fight was furious but brief. Nasir stepped over the body with cold satisfaction to meet the next bandit coming at him. He fought for his life on the bloodstained sand. But while he did his best to avoid being killed, while he kept an eye on his men, while he glanced from time to time to the blockade around the core camp to make sure the bandits weren't breaching that, he was aware of Majid's position and, encounter by encounter, made his way toward his cousin.

SADIE GRABBED another strip of cloth and rolled it up, glancing at the water boiling on the low fire. She would have given anything for a few bottles of liquor to use as disinfectant, but since Islam forbade alcohol, there probably wouldn't be any of that in camp, even if she knew how to ask for it. Using hand signals, she asked the women to tear up more cloth for bandages.

"*Shukran,*" she thanked them with a smile and moved to the tent entrance to glance out.

The sounds of battle were terrifying. She had to force herself to stay standing, every instinct compelling her to lie flat on the sand. She couldn't see much from the blockade. The men were fighting outside it now.

Where was Nasir?

Why weren't the wounded coming back for treatment?

She could see men on the ground out there, recognized several who belonged to the camp. Yet none of them made a single move toward help, toward safety. On some level, she understood that their honor probably prevented them from leaving the battle. As a doctor, she was angry and frustrated at not being able to help them. She could. She still could, if only they came to her. But the injured she could see stayed where they'd fallen, fighting until their last breath.

Nasir could be hurt. He could be lying somewhere, fighting like that, dying. *Or already dead.* Her head spun at the thought.

Instinct pushed her to go out and drag the injured in one by one, but she had few illusions about what would happen if she did. She would be shot before she reached the first.

It wasn't fear that stopped her, but the practicality of her medical training. If Nasir won, she could wait until the battle was over and save many. If he lost, Majid's men would kill them all anyhow.

She looked toward the tent next to hers. The flap there, too, was open a slit, a woman watching, worrying for a husband or a son, someone she loved.

She heard Nasir's voice ring out over the din of battle and her chest expanded to fill with air. *He is still alive.* She wished she could see him. Instead she spotted a man slip between the cars of the barricade. Close on his heels came another—Nasir's men both and more following behind. Retreating, she realized when she saw the enemy pour in after them.

The level of noise rose in the tent. The women, some of whom watched the battle through gaps in the side panels, understood what was happening. A few prayed out loud now, others cried as they held on to their children.

Sadie turned her attention back to what was going on outside, holding her breath for Nasir to appear. He was the last in his tribe to pull back, shouting to his men, giving orders as he fought like a lion.

There were fewer gunshots now. Most clips were empty, and there was no time to reload. The fighting was done with daggers or bare hands, rifles used like clubs to smash skulls, shoulders and kneecaps.

The men of the tribe were badly outnumbered. Nasir held off two men as a third was sneaking up behind him.

She shouted, but it didn't seem her warning reached that far.

Lord, don't let him be hurt. Not Nasir.

Where was a damn weapon? She pulled back and looked around, frantic with desperation. The tent held nothing useful for fighting other than a few sharp knives she had disinfected over the flames earlier in case she needed to perform emergency surgery.

She grabbed one of these now and some of the other women did the same, a few holding their cooking knives as they pushed their children behind them, waiting for the enemy to reach the tent.

Then they were there, the first of them falling backward through a ripped side panel. More came and the boiling water was upset, scalding one of the men. Booted feet kicked sand over the fire.

The women huddled in the corners, clutching their knives, but the men, fighting their way through the tent, paid little attention to them. Sadie grabbed for the rolls of bandages being trampled into the wet sand. All her work to create a semiclean environment where she could treat the wounded was now ruined. She watched for Nasir—several of the side panels had been torn off—and caught sight of him in the thick of the fighting.

The men finally passed through her tent. Some of the women, Sadie noticed suddenly and with surprise, were now finishing off the fallen enemy, cutting a man's neck with the same skill as they butchered live-stock for dinner.

She saw Nasir again and her heart stopped. He was injured. He'd fallen to one knee in the sand, but was holding off his at-tackers with a knife. And the next thing she knew she was running toward him without even making a conscious decision.

The realization that she was unarmed hit her—she'd dropped her knife when she'd tried to save the bandages—but she didn't care. She fell on one of the bandits from behind, took him to the ground with the force of her lunge rather than by strength, catching him off balance.

"Go back," Nasir shouted next to her.

She couldn't respond. The man she fought was getting the upper hand, requiring all her focus and strength. She ended up on the bottom somehow, the man's knees on her chest. He was choking her with one hand, using the other to hold together a gaping hole on his arm. Blood ran through her fingers, dripping on her face. She couldn't breathe.

From the corner of her eyes she saw Nasir thrust his knife into the heart of the man he fought, but as soon as he shoved the body away, another one of Majid's men came at him.

She kicked the bandit who held her down—to keep his attention from her hands—then reached for the gun of the man Nasir had just finished. She squeezed the trigger, barely taking the time to aim.

The bandit let go of her and clutched his stomach with both hands, and when she shoved, he fell to the side without resistance. He did not get up.

She sat, dizzy and nauseous. Nasir was just finishing with his latest attacker. He struggled to his feet and came for her, pulled her up, pulled her with him into the cover of a tent that was still standing, apart from the center of fighting. Then he turned to leave her.

"No. Stay. You're injured." She grabbed after him.

He was covered in blood, hard to say what was others' and what was his own. A few open wounds still seeped. He needed immediate disinfection and serious stitching. She glanced toward the tent she'd set up as a field hospital, now a jumble of carpets trampled into the sand. She looked back at him. His face seemed pale. How much blood had he lost? "Are you dizzy? Weak?"

He shook his head and flashed her a smile as he reloaded his gun. "I'm Bedu."

She supposed that translated as something like, "I was born to be strong." She scanned what she could see of his wounds. Did he have any internal injuries? If so, his blood pressure would be going down. He wasn't showing any sign of that.

He leaned closer and grabbed her by the shoulders. "Stay safe. For me." He kissed her so fiercely, it made her go weak in the knees all over again.

She clung to him, not wanting to let him go, but he broke away and rushed back into the fight with a cry, limping, bleeding and somehow looking terrifyingly glorious.

THEY'D BEEN CIRCLING each other for hours and now met in the middle of the battle, each armed with nothing but a dagger.

"Today you die, dog." Majid spat on the sand, his face distorted with hatred. "And the bastards of your godless brother die with you. Everyone of your blood will be erased today."

So that was why he had ridden for the camp instead of staying with the bulk of his troops. Nasir grabbed his weapon tighter. Majid had thought Saeed had sent the children to the desert to hide them.

He wanted the children. Nasir thought of Salah, his bright, mischievous nephew; the twin girls who already had their mother's beauty at age three; Aziz, a baby, barely born. Majid would kill them all.

Rage propelled him forward, and they met in a bone-rattling crash, blade clanging against blade.

Neither gave. They were evenly matched in strength, although Nasir had more injuries. His cousin, he discovered after a moment, wore a light bulletproof vest under his robes. His dagger could not penetrate anything vital. He could do no real damage.

He had to go for the throat, his only chance to stop the man. They clashed again, got locked into a position from which neither could move any longer, broke apart.

He watched, calculating as they circled each other. Each movement hurt, each breath threatened to burst his labored lungs. He could not slow down, he could not lose. If he died, everyone he loved would die with him.

His eyes locked with Majid's for a moment then the man's gaze slid to somewhere behind him. Nasir didn't have the chance to spin around. The gun that discharged close by rendered him deaf. Then came the pain, and he felt his legs give way as the dagger dropped from his hand. Burning, bone-splitting pain seared through him.

He hit the sand, and for a moment the pain intensified. Then he felt nothing, saw nothing.

Chapter Eleven

Sadie treated the injured the best she could in the single tent still standing. A few of the children and the women had been hit by stray bullets. Wives were dragging their fallen husbands to her and Shadia. The tent was filling up quickly, thick with the smell of blood and death.

She removed bullets and set bones. Shadia stitched wounds and administered some concoction of hers for pain relief. It seemed to work remarkably well. When this was all over, she wanted to ask Nasir to translate the ingredients for her.

When the noise of fighting lessened outside, hope rose in her. She wanted to go to the flap and look out, look for Nasir, but she couldn't stop what she was doing, not for a minute.

She just finished dressing a head injury when a woman rushed in and let out a long cry, then talked so fast and full of emotion that the sound barely resembled human language. The other women in the tent grabbed up their children and rushed out, several motioning her to follow, their expressions full of fear and urgency. They shouted to her; one grabbed her and yanked her toward the exit forcefully. She pulled her arm away and shook her head. She had to stay with her patients. The woman said something again, but did not wait any longer. She looked around, but could not find Shadia. When had she left?

Within a few seconds she was alone, except for the critically injured. She knew something terrible was about to happen, that the fight was lost, but she could not leave those she was supposed to care for. The wail of a child rose somewhere in the corner. Another answered the next second. She went to investigate and found two small girls and a boy behind a large water jar.

Where was their mother? Dead perhaps. She tried to pick them up, but could not hold all three. She grabbed the girls—they were smallest—placed one on each hip and ducked out of the tent. She could see the women and children running for the dunes in disarray.

Where was Nasir?

She took a tentative step back toward the injured that lay scattered over the sand, but she realized she could do nothing to help them, not now. She spun and ran toward the desert, focused on saving the children. She caught up with the stragglers, handed over the girls then spun around and rushed back for the little boy. She nearly reached the tent when one of the bandits spotted her and came after her.

She was fast, but he was faster. The butt of a gun slammed into the back of her neck, sending her sprawling. The blade of a knife flashed in front of her face, descending in a swoop. A single word, barked somewhere close, stopped it.

She swallowed, lying on her side, as the grinning face of the bandit left her field of vision, replaced by another man.

"Umman." She said his name and scampered to sit.

"Nasir's foreign whore." The man's eyes were cold with hate. "The queen's latest friend. Would she have the gates opened for you?"

A few seconds passed before she gained the meaning of his words—the palace gates. He meant to use her as hostage to gain admittance to the royal palace.

"No!" she said, but was ignored and pulled to her feet roughly by one of Umman's men.

She was shoved forward, forced to march over the sand back toward camp, through the bodies of the fallen. She desperately searched the ground, praying not to find Nasir.

But she did see him, lying still in his own blood. Shadia kneeled next to him, her head covered with her hands as she wailed.

A glimpse was all Sadie got before tears flooded her eyes, as pain flooded her heart. Nasir was hurt—seriously so. She fought with all she had, but the men dragged her up to the back of a pickup and tied her down in a corner.

She cranked her neck, blinking the tears

of worry and rage away, watching Shadia dab at the blood on Nasir's face. What was going on? Was he dying?

Had they killed him? They would have, wouldn't they? Majid wouldn't leave him behind otherwise. The ropes cut into her flesh as she strained against them. Nasir was likely dead, and she was only alive to be used as a pawn against the king and queen.

Dimly, she thought that she ought to do something, but she could not act, could barely move from the grief that pressed down on her, suffocating her as effectively as quicksand.

HE WANTED TO DIE, but someone wouldn't let him.

Nasir opened his eyes and found Shadia leaning over him, the cool of a metal cup pressed against his lips.

"Drink," she said, her voice barely audible over the ululating of the women that filtered in from outside.

His tribe was mourning. He saw grim-faced men through the open flap, men from the other camps of his tribe—when had they arrived?—who were helping to erect tents that had been trampled, others gathering up the dead.

"Drink."

He didn't have the strength to resist the foul brew that made him cough. He tried to turn his head, the motion bringing a new wave of suffering. "Sadie?" He pushed the single word through his parched lips.

The old woman took the opportunity and sloshed some more liquid in. "Gone," she said. "They took her."

Fear, rage and purpose rose inside him all at once. He lifted his hand, tipped the cup and drank more.

"The others?" he asked after he pulled away.

"Many dead." She listed the names, and each was a blow, each a friend, a member of the family, a man he had been responsible for.

"Insallah." Shadia wiped his brow. "God willed it."

He lay back onto the bloodstained carpet and closed his eyes, fought against the pain. He thought of each and every man, what he owed to the fallen, to their families. Then he thought of Sadie and his teeth clenched, the walls of his chest caving in, crushing his lungs and his heart.

Majid had her.

When the breathtaking pain of that subsided a little, he opened his eyes again. "What's broken?" He tentatively moved his limbs. They felt weak, but other than his head, he experienced no shooting pain.

"Allah kept your bones whole, Sheik." Shadia lifted the cup to his lips again. "The injury is to your head alone." She drew a light finger across the right side of his forehead that was on fire. "Your blood poured out for your people. You must rest," she said. "You must gain back the blood and your strength."

No, he thought, *I must gain back my heart.*

THE BANDITS CAMPED for the night and were now sleeping or lounging around the fires. They had little to fear, Sadie supposed. They'd just about annihilated Nasir's men.

Nasir.

The last time she'd seen him, he'd been lying in blood on the battlefield. In the desperation of the moment she'd thought him dead, but now, looking back, she wondered. She had not been close enough to see his injuries. Was it possible, could there be the faintest chance that he was alive? Or was she now repainting the picture, her mind desperate to come up with some hope that the man she'd fallen in love with hadn't been killed?

She loved him.

It seemed a cruel twist of fate to realize that now, too late.

*But if it wasn't...*hope whispered in her ear, ignoring reason.

If he was alive, then she had to get to him somehow to help.

She had to escape—for Nasir and the rest of his people. She could not allow Majid to use her as a pawn. She had to brave the desert.

Images of her last ill-fated escape came to mind, and her chest tightened at the thought of quicksand. She took a deep breath, then another. She would follow the tracks Majid's men left and go back to Nasir's camp with the children. That path had to be safe. And the sand was so marked up by the rebels' cars that they might not notice her footprints, or might not notice it long enough for her to reach camp.

She listened to the night. The men had not set up tents, but had bunked down on the sand next to the cars. Thirty of the initial fifty bandits remained. Umman among them. And Majid. She had heard the name spoken and figured out it belonged to the man who was now sitting by one of the fires, yelling at two others.

Somewhere nearby the rest of Majid's forces fought with the king's army. She had no doubt that at first light they would be marching to join them.

She lay with her back braced against the tire of a pickup. Umman lay in front of her, a little over a foot of sand between them, Majid's men all around. Everyone but the night guards seemed to be asleep.

She reached forward with infinite slowness, hesitated a split second before touching her fingertips to the hilt of Umman's dagger. She held her breath. He didn't move. She withdrew the weapon a fraction of an inch at a time, silently, until it was hers. She wasted no time, bending to her feet, to her left ankle that had been tied with a rope and secured to the pickup's bumper.

She put the blade to the rope and stopped to listen, but could hear nothing other than the faint sounds of snoring. Nobody stirred as she began sawing the fibers. She did it a little at a time, stopping frequently to look around. Then the rope gave and she pushed it off, wiggled her body to the gap between the two tires, hoping to climb through under the truck to the other side.

She was half-in half-out when Umman turned. His eyes popped open and he rose. She darted forward, one hand pressed against his mouth, the other thrusting the blade into his heart. His body jerked once, then went limp. She laid him onto the sand and pulled his water flask off his belt, then backed under the pickup again, pushed through and peeked out the other side.

Two night guards sat in the sand a hundred yards to her left with their backs to her. They were there to watch for outside attack so they paid little attention to the camp. She used that advantage and crept in the opposite direction.

She crawled on her stomach toward the five-foot-wide indentation the pickups had left in the sand, clearly visible in the moonlight. When she reached it, she stayed on the track, stayed low until she went over the first higher dune. Then she straightened, and after a quick glance behind her to make sure nobody could see her now, she started into a sprint.

When she got winded, about a half an hour or so later, she slowed. A balmy breeze from the south blew sand over the tracks, but not enough to cover them. An hour later, however, the wind strengthened. She could still see the groove of tires here and there, but more and more she was forced to navigate by guesswork. Another hour after that, she was good and truly lost.

NASIR RODE with a hundred men toward the main battle, expecting Majid to be heading there with his hostage.

He had to get Sadie back.

His *fakhadh*'s pickups had been taken by the enemy; only the ones that had caught on fire in the fight or had been shot up to the point of uselessness had been left behind. He and the few men who'd survived the battle at camp rode camels—and their camels were bred for speed. Outnumbering them ten to one were cars and pickups that had brought dozens of fighters from the rest of his tribe that morning, all coming to their sheik's side.

His men flew over the sand all around him. They could hear the sounds of gunfire now, but couldn't yet see the battle fought in a rocky area of the desert where the rolling land obstructed view. Then they came around a string of boulders and could see before them the desperate fight.

Beharrain's army had been divided. Some of the troops stood in a ring around the capital, guarding Tihrin, and border forces had been strengthened, too, in case any of the country's neighbors thought the breakout of rebel fighting provided a good opportunity to lay claim to territories rich in oil. The force sent to the desert was a fair match for Majid's bandits, who seemed to number more than had been previously estimated.

Nasir raised his rifle and squeezed a series of shots into the air, shouting the Bedu battle cry as he urged Ronu into a flat-out run to join the fight. But just as he did so, he spotted a group of pickups coming into view from the east—Majid's smaller band. He turned Ronu and charged toward them, slipping to the sand from the saddle when he was close enough.

The fight was as brief as it was bloody. His men fought like djinni who had powers beyond that of mortals. One bandit fell after the other. Then finally Nasir was face-to-face with Majid.

"Where is she?" Nasir asked as he charged.

"Dead," Majid spat the word.

All the world went black for Nasir, save for the man in front of him, the noise of the battle in his ears, the smell of blood in his nostrils.

He moved without conscious thought or effort, his blade slicing into his enemy. He could not feel any injury of his own. There was no room for sensation in his body other than grief and rage. A terrible howl swirled around him, and only after some time did he realize that the sound had issued forth from his own mouth.

He stabbed, cut and pushed forward, relentlessly, on and on. He didn't stop until the bastard was dead, lying in blood, lifeless at his feet.

Nasir's chest heaved with effort and pain as he looked to the fight that raged a hundred meters ahead. Majid's bandits had seen their leader fall and were already faltering, the royal army gaining the upper hand. The battle was decided.

Ronu found him and nudged his face. Nasir sheathed his blade as the camel knelt without having to be told. He pulled himself into the saddle, only now noticing that Majid had cut him in several spots.

He looked at the battle one last time. Some of Majid's men were already running. He had no taste to hunt them. Let the army take care of it.

He turned Ronu into the direction from where Majid's men had arrived to the fight and followed their tracks. He had arrived too late to save Sadie, but he would at least retrieve her body. He could not let her be found by the desert scavengers. If he couldn't keep her safe in life, his honor and his broken heart demanded that he keep her safe in death.

He rode, his eyes sharp on the desert, the rest of his body numb.

He thought of her courage at Umman's bandit camp, her wisdom at the palace when they'd been looking for the spies, her passion in his arms up in the garden. He had found a pearl among women, the love of his heart. And he had lost her.

After some time, he came across the spot where the men had camped for the night. Noon came, the sun merciless above, but he did not stop to rest in Ronu's shade. He rode around in widening circles.

He was dizzy from heat when he spotted something dark and small on the horizon, had to look twice to make sure his eyes weren't merely playing a trick on him. But no, there was something there. He urged Ronu into a gallop.

Eventually the small black dot grew into a form. A woman wearing the *abayah*. A woman standing, walking away from him. A woman very much alive.

He urged Ronu faster until he had to hang on to the saddle so he wouldn't fall out. Then he was close enough for the woman to hear the hoofbeats and she turned. *Sadie.*

Was it a mirage? Was the desert showing him the desire of his heart, like it sometimes showed large lakes ahead to those who wandered its arid dunes dying from thirst? Was it a trick of the eyes?

Ronu closed the distance between them as fast as if he were running a race, and when they neared, Nasir slid from the saddle without waiting for the camel to come to a full stop.

She was real.

"Sadie!"

"Nasir." She cried his name as she flew into his arms. "You're safe."

He held her tight. They stood speechless,

their arms wrapped around each other, for an eternity. She was safe. *Safe. Alive.*

"I have you whole," he said, and kissed her without patience, needing to feel her, to touch her to believe.

SADIE WATCHED the sun rise over the desert, filled to the brim with the beauty of it. Sara, Abu's wife, was talking rapidly in Arabic with smiling eyes. She was happy to catch one word in every ten, but she made out the general meaning. Sara was once again telling her how happy she was to have Sadie as her honorary daughter.

Abu and Sara had had nine sons. They lost one in the battle. Sadie had saved the life of three who'd been critically injured. Since the family had no daughters they'd asked her through Nasir if she would accept them. She'd done so gladly. It resolved the problem of where she would stay until the wedding. Dara, of course, invited her to the palace, but she didn't want to leave Nasir and she didn't want to leave those in camp who still needed her help, although Shadia was working miracles with her ancient cures.

Sara reached for her hand and pulled her back from the opening of the tent. She led her to a pillow and motioned for her to sit down, then produced some dark liquid and a brush and began to paint Sadie's face, a line down her chin, something between her eyebrows. She figured the liquid for henna and stayed still, submitting herself to local custom, sitting calmly while Sara drew extensive designs on her hands and feet.

"*Shukran.*" She smiled as she thanked Sara when it was done.

The woman smiled back and nodded, but when Sadie moved to rise, she pushed her back with a gentle hand. She brought a saddlebag from the corner and upended it on the carpet in front of her.

"Oh… Wow." Sadie could do nothing but stare at the jewelry that spilled forth. Earrings and necklaces, gold belts, all manner of body ornaments more elaborate than she had ever seen covered the carpet, all created with superb workmanship. Sara nodded approvingly as she dug through them and selected a pair of dangly earrings and handed them to her.

"Where did these come from?" She didn't think the average Bedu camped with millions in jewels and precious gems tucked under the carpets. "Dara?" Had the queen sent this for her to borrow for the wedding?

"Sadie," Sara said and selected a necklace that consisted of a dozen strands, each longer than the other, and put it around Sadie's neck herself. The necklace covered her from neck to solar plexus, the gold decorated with turquoise.

Next, Sara brought a silk headdress, a shade lighter than the *abayah* Sadie wore, and fastened that with another piece of matching jewelry that sat on Sadie's head like an old-fashioned crown.

After she finished off the look with a half a pound of bracelets on each arm, she took Sadie's hand and led her outside the tent where Abu and his sons were waiting. One of them held Ronu's rope. The camel was decorated with carpets and tassels, his rein braided with gold.

"*Shukran,*" she said as they helped her up.

The whole camp seemed to have gathered

around by this time, the whole tribe even. They'd been feasting here for several days now, in anticipation of their sheik's wedding. Dara and Saeed hadn't come—Saeed was still recovering and Aziz was too young to travel—but they'd sent outrageous presents along with an invitation to the palace for a big celebration there. Her mother would be meeting them in Tihrin with her new boyfriend to finally meet her son-in-law and his family. She'd decided to skip the desert. She didn't know what she was missing.

Sadie settled in the saddle, hoping that Ronu wouldn't be led all around camp, which had grown considerably to make room for the visitors. If so, she wouldn't reach Nasir for another half a day. But thankfully, her new father and brothers led the camel straight to Nasir's tent—his new tent, as regal as the one in the tent room in the palace, a wedding gift from Dara and Saeed.

He stood in front of it with his male relatives, all dressed in their finest. But none looked as fine as Nasir in a gorgeous white robe and headdress, a golden dagger stuck into his belt.

The women of the camp ululated and sang as Sadie slipped from the camel, touching the ground in front of Nasir.

"Welcome to our tent," he said and led her inside.

The noise level doubled as the tent flap closed behind them, everyone shouting, "*Mabruk!*" Good luck. On top of that, several rifles were fired into the air.

"Is it done?" she asked.

"I've announced it three times in front of the elders. According to our customs, we are married," he said. And then he kissed her.

Each time he'd kissed her before it had been an experience that shook her to her core, melted her. This kiss claimed her body and captured her heart. The world spun with her, and she realized just how much he had held back until now. His passion was a palpable presence that filled the tent.

"I love you," he said against her lips a long while later. "*Ya noori.* You are my light."

"I love you."

He kissed her again, tasting of jasmine tea

and passion. "Nice dowry," he said once he made his way to her neck and nudged aside the sizable earring she wore.

"Dowry?" she mumbled, her mind in a haze.

"It's customary for the father to give some of the bride price back as dowry."

"Bride price?" She was trying to pay attention, but he was lowering her to the carpets and his hands and mouth felt too wonderful to think of anything else. Still, the thought surfaced again a little later. "You paid for me?"

He looked up, his gaze burning with heat. "A queen's ransom," he said. "Twenty camels, including Ronu, a tent, half the jewels from my grandfather's raiding days—" He nibbled his way back to her mouth as he spoke.

"Not Ronu!" Her brain caught up with his words.

"It seems Abu sent him back as part of your dowry as well, of course…" His voiced trailed off as he tasted her bottom lip.

"Of course what?" She tried not to melt into a puddle of incoherence.

"It means Ronu is yours now. A Bedu woman maintains possession of her dowry. It does not pass into the hands of her husband."

"I'll let you ride him now and then."

"We'll ride him together." He said the words with a wicked smile that made her think of a particular mural at that ancient pleasure palace. Her pulse quickened.

His hand found its way under her dress, and that was the end of conversation on Bedu property rights. She was unable to think of anything else but the way his probing fingers felt on her skin.

He freed her from her clothes one piece at a time, allowing the silk to slide off her body in a caress, kissing every inch of skin as it was bared.

"Among our people it is the groom's duty to undress his bride. If a bride were to undress herself, she might be considered wanton by her husband," he said as he pulled off her tunic, the last piece of clothing she had on.

Being undressed by Nasir was the most erotic experience she had ever had.

"And if I turn out to be a wanton wife after all?" she asked, wearing nothing but the jewelry, feeling like Cleopatra.

"Considering your foreign upbringing, it would be understandable," he said with pretend chagrin, struggling to hold back a grin. "In that case, I will live with my burden."

She kissed him then, showing him just how wanton she could be, how much he had aroused her. When they needed to break for air, he dipped his lips to her nipple and tasted her skin, sending jolts of pleasure skittering through her body. Her half-closed eyelids fluttered open when he pulled his dagger close. There had better not be some barbaric custom of wedding nights that included sharp blades. But before she could voice her concern, he pulled a pottery jar from behind a rolled up carpet and popped the wax seal with the blade before discarding it. He dipped a finger into the jar and lifted it to her lips.

"What is it?" she asked, but was already reaching her tongue to taste what looked like honey. Honey with a twist, she realized as the flavor spread through her mouth.

"Spiced wild honey," he said and licked the remainder off his finger before reaching into the jar for more. "Mussafa Pasha's favorite dessert."

She wouldn't have thought she could have become more aroused, but the way Nasir was looking at her as he raised his finger to drip honey over her nipples sent her body soaring. The taste of the honey was sweet and spicy on her tongue. She could identify cinnamon, but could not name any of the other spices that now heated her skin, creating a tingling effect, which increased as Nasir's hot mouth enclosed her hardened bud.

He drew on her gently at first, then harder, his honeyed fingers rolling her other nipple between them. Heat gathered low in the V of her thighs. She pressed herself against the hard body next to her, blindly seeking release. Nasir answered by drizzling more honey over her still, following its path down, licking it from her skin, from her belly button, his tongue doing a seductive dance that drove her mad with need.

"I thought we could ride back to the pleasure palace and spend a few days there, discover Mussaffa's secrets," he said as he pulled up her knees, spread them and positioned himself between them. But he would not give all of himself to her, not yet. He scooped more of the spiced honey and drip by drip coated her innermost parts with it and feasted on her until she was sucked under and drowned in pleasure, her body contracting and pulsating against him.

Only then did he lift her hips and take her with slow thrusts that stoked her fire to roaring flames again. She had never felt as alive as she did in this moment. As loved. As cherished. She felt herself constrict around him, and at the hot spurt of his own release, she called his name on a voice drunk with pleasure.

His dark gaze burned with love as he raised his head to look at her. "You are as beautiful as rain," he said.

And she understood what that meant to a Bedu of the desert. He possessed poetry, after all, she thought, loving him, feeling loved in return, beyond measure.

* * * * *

Experience entertaining women's fiction for every woman who has wondered "what's next?" in her life.
Turn the page for a sneak preview of a new book from Harlequin NEXT,
WHY IS MURDER ON THE MENU, ANYWAY?
by Stevi Mittman

On sale December 26, wherever books are sold.

Design Tip of the Day

> Ambience is everything. Imagine eating a foie gras at a luncheonette counter or a side of coleslaw at Le Cirque. It's not a matter of food but one of atmosphere. Remember that when planning your dining room design.
>
> —Tips from *Teddi.com*

"Now that's the kind of man you should be looking for," my mother, the self-appointed keeper of my shelf-life stamp, says. She points with her fork at a man in the corner of the Steak-Out Restaurant, a dive I've just been hired to redecorate. Making this restaurant look four-star will be hard, but not half as hard as getting through lunch without strangling the woman across the table from me. "*He* would make a good husband."

"Oh, you can tell that from across the room?" I ask, wondering how it is she can forget that when we had trouble getting rid of my last husband, she shot him. "Besides being ten minutes away from death if he actually eats all that steak, he's twenty years too old for me and—shallow woman that I am—twenty pounds too heavy. Besides, I am *so* not looking for another husband here. I'm looking to design a new image for this place, looking for some sense of ambience, some feeling, something I can build a proposal on for them."

My mother studies the man in the corner, tilting her head, the better to gauge his age, I suppose. I think she's grimacing, but with all the Botox and Restylane injected into that face, it's hard to tell. She takes another bite of her steak, chews slowly so that I don't miss the fact that the steak is a poor cut and tougher than it should be. "You're concentrating on the wrong kind of proposal," she says finally. "Just look at this place, Teddi. It's a dive. There are hardly any other diners. What does *that* tell you about the food?"

"That they cater to a dinner crowd and it's lunchtime," I tell her.

I don't know what I was thinking bringing her here with me. I suppose I thought it would be better than eating alone. There really are days when my common sense goes on vacation. Clearly, this is one of them. I mean really, did I not resolve less than three weeks ago that I would not let my mother get to me anymore?

What good are New Year's resolutions, anyway?

Mario approaches the man's table and my mother studies him while they converse. Eventually Mario leaves the table with a huff, after which the diner glances up and meets my mother's gaze. I think she's smiling at him. That or she's got indigestion. They size each other up.

I concentrate on making sketches in my

notebook and try to ignore the fact that my mother is flirting. At nearly seventy, she's developed an unhealthy interest in members of the opposite sex to whom she isn't married.

According to my father, who has broken the TMI rule and given me Too Much Information, she has no interest in sex with him. Better, I suppose, to be clued in on what they aren't doing in the bedroom than have to hear what they might be doing.

"He's not so old," my mother says, noticing that I have barely touched the Chinese chicken salad she warned me not to get. "He's got about as many years on you as you have on your little cop friend."

She does this to make me crazy. I know it, but it works all the same. "Drew Scoones is not my little 'friend.' He's a detective with whom I—"

"Screwed around," my mother says. I must look shocked, because my mother laughs at me and asks if I think she doesn't know the "lingo."

What I thought she didn't know was that Drew and I actually tangled in the sheets.

And, since it's possible she's just fishing, I sidestep the issue and tell her that Drew is just a couple of years younger than me and that I don't need reminding. I dig into my salad with renewed vigor, determined to show my mother that Chinese chicken salad in a steak place was not the stupid choice it's proving to be.

After a few more minutes of my picking at the wilted leaves on my plate, the man my mother has me nearly engaged to pays his bill and heads past us toward the back of the restaurant. I watch my mother take in his shoes, his suit and the diamond pinkie ring that seems to be cutting off the circulation in his little finger.

"Such nice hands," she says after the man is out of sight. "Manicured." She and I both stare at my hands. I have two popped acrylics that are being held on at weird angles by bandages. My cuticles are ragged and there's marker decorating my right hand from measuring carelessly when I did a drawing for a customer.

Twenty minutes later she's disappointed that he managed to leave the restaurant without our noticing. He will join the list of the ones I let get away. I will hear about him twenty years from now when—according to my mother—my children will be grown and I will still be single, living pathetically alone with several dogs and cats.

After my ex, that sounds good to me.

The waitress tells us that our meal has been taken care of by the management and, after thanking Mario, the owner, complimenting him on the wonderful meal and assuring him that once I have redecorated his place people will be flocking here in droves (I actually use those words and ignore my mother when she rolls her eyes), my mother and I head for the restroom.

My father—unfortunately not with us today—has the patience of a saint. He got it over the years of living with my mother. She, perhaps as a result, figures he has the patience for both of them, and feels justified having none. For her, no rules apply, and a little thing like a picture of a man on the door to a public restroom is certainly no barrier to using the john. In all fairness, it does seem silly to stand and wait for the ladies' room if no one is using the men's room.

Still, it's the idea that rules don't apply to her, signs don't apply to her, conventions don't apply to her. She knocks on the door to the men's room. When no one answers she gestures to me to go in ahead. I tell her that I can certainly wait for the ladies' room to be free and she shrugs and goes in herself.

Not a minute later there is a bloodcurdling scream from behind the men's room door.

"Mom!" I yell. "Are you all right?"

Mario comes running over, the waitress on his heels. Two customers head our way while my mother continues to scream.

I try the door, but it is locked. I yell for her to open it and she fumbles with the knob. When she finally manages to unlock and open it, she is white behind her two streaks of blush, but she is on her feet and appears shaken but not stirred.

"What happened?" I ask her. So do Mario and the waitress and the few customers who have migrated to the back of the place.

She points toward the bathroom and I go

in, thinking it serves her right for using the men's room. But I see nothing amiss.

She gestures toward the stall, and, like any self-respecting and suspicious woman, I poke the door open with one finger, expecting the worst.

What I find is worse than the worst.

The husband my mother picked out for me is sitting on the toilet. His pants are puddled around his ankles, his hands are hanging at his sides. Pinned to his chest is some sort of Health Department certificate.

Oh, and there is a large, round, bloodless bullet hole between his eyes.

Four Nassau County police officers are securing the area, waiting for the detectives and crime scene personnel to show up. They are trying, though not very hard, to comfort my mother, who in another era would be considered to be suffering from the vapors. Less tactful in the twenty-first century, I'd say she was losing it. That is, if I didn't know her better, know she was milking it for everything it was worth.

My mother loves attention. As it begins to

flag, she swoons and claims to feel faint. Despite four No Smoking signs, my mother insists it's all right for her to light up because, after all, she's in shock. Not to mention that signs, as we know, don't apply to her.

When asked not to smoke, she collapses mournfully in a chair and lets her head loll to the side, all without mussing her hair.

Eventually, the detectives show up to find the four patrolmen all circled around her, debating whether to administer CPR, smelling salts or simply call the paramedics. I, however, know just what will snap her to attention.

"Detective Scoones," I say loudly. My mother parts the sea of cops.

"We have to stop meeting like this," he says lightly to me, but I can feel him checking me over with his eyes, making sure I'm all right while pretending not to care.

"What have you got in those pants?" my mother asks him, coming to her feet and staring at his crotch accusingly. "*Baydar?* Everywhere we Bayers are, you turn up.

You don't expect me to buy that this is a coincidence, I hope."

Drew tells my mother that it's nice to see her, too, and asks if it's his fault that her daughter seems to attract disasters.

Charming to be made to feel like the bearer of a plague.

He asks how I am.

"Just peachy," I tell him. "I seem to be making a habit of finding dead bodies, my mother is driving me crazy and the catering hall I booked two freakin' years ago for Dana's bat mitzvah has just been shut down by the Board of Health!"

"Glad to see your luck's finally changing," he says, giving me a quick squeeze around the shoulders before turning his attention to the patrolmen, asking what they've got, whether they've taken any statements, moved anything, all the sort of stuff you see on TV, without any of the drama. That is, if you don't count my mother's threats to faint every few minutes when she senses no one's paying attention to her.

Mario tells his waitstaff to bring everyone espresso, which I decline because I'm wired enough. Drew pulls him aside and a minute later I'm handed a cup of coffee that smells divinely of Kahlúa.

The man knows me well. Too well.

His partner, whom I've met once or twice, says he'll interview the kitchen staff. Drew asks Mario if he minds if he takes statements from the patrons first and gets to him and the waitstaff afterward.

"No, no," Mario tells him. "Do the patrons first." Drew raises his eyebrow at me like he wants to know if I get the double entendre. I try to look bored.

"What is it with you and murder victims?" he asks me when we sit down at a table in the corner.

I search them out so that I can see you again, I almost say, but I'm afraid it will sound desperate instead of sarcastic.

My mother, lighting up and daring him with a look to tell her not to, reminds him that *she* was the one to find the body.

Drew asks what happened *this time*. My mother tells him how the man in the john was "taken" with me, couldn't take his eyes off me and blatantly flirted with both of us.

To his credit, Drew doesn't laugh, but his smirk is undeniable to the trained eye. And I've had my eye trained on him for nearly a year now.

"While he was noticing you," he asks me, "did *you* notice anything about him? Was he waiting for anyone? Watching for anything?"

I tell him that he didn't appear to be waiting or watching. That he made no phone calls, was fairly intent on eating and did, indeed, flirt with my mother. This last bit Drew takes with a grain of salt, which was the way it was intended.

"And he had a short conversation with Mario," I tell him. "I think he might have been unhappy with the food, though he didn't send it back."

Drew asks what makes me think he was dissatisfied, and I tell him that the discussion seemed acrimonious and that Mario looked distressed when he left the table. Drew makes a note and says he'll look into it and asks about anyone else in the restaurant. Did I see anyone who didn't seem to belong, anyone who was watching the victim, anyone looking suspicious?

"Besides my mother?" I ask him, and Mom huffs and blows her cigarette smoke in my direction.

I tell him that there were several deliveries, the kitchen staff going in and out the back door to grab a smoke. He stops me and asks what I was doing checking out the back door of the restaurant.

Proudly—because, while he was off forgetting me, dropping by only once in a while to say hi to Jesse, my son, or drop something by for one of my daughters that he thought they might like, I was getting on with my life—I tell him that I'm decorating the place.

He looks genuinely impressed. "Commercial customers? That's great," he says. Okay, that's what he *ought* to say. What he actually says is "Whatever pays the bills."

"Howard Rosen, the famous restaurant critic, got her the job," my mother says. "You met him—the good-looking, distinguished gentleman with the *real* job, something to be proud of. I guess you've never read his reviews in *Newsday*."

Drew, without missing a beat, tells her

that Howard's reviews are on the top of his list, as soon as he learns how to read.

"I only meant—" my mother starts, but both of us assure her that we know just what she meant.

"So," Drew says. "Deliveries?"

I tell him that Mario would know better than I, but that I saw vegetables come in, maybe fish and linens.

"This is the second restaurant job Howard's got her," my mother tells Drew.

"At least she's getting *something* out of the relationship," he says.

"If he were here," my mother says, ignoring the insinuation, "he'd be comforting her instead of interrogating her. He'd be making sure we're both all right after such an ordeal."

"I'm sure he would," Drew agrees, then looks me in the eyes as if he's measuring my tolerance for shock. Quietly he adds, "But then maybe he doesn't know just what strong stuff your daughter's made of."

It's the closest thing to a tender moment I can expect from Drew Scoones. My mother breaks the spell. "She gets that from me," she says.

Both Drew and I take a minute, probably to pray that's all I inherited from her.

"I'm just trying to save you some time and effort," my mother tells him. "My money's on Howard."

Drew withers her with a look and mutters something that sounds suspiciously like "fool's gold." Then he excuses himself to go back to work.

I catch his sleeve and ask if it's all right for us to leave. He says sure, he knows where we live. I say goodbye to Mario. I assure him that I will have some sketches for him in a few days, all the while hoping that this murder doesn't cancel his redecorating plans. I need the money desperately, the alternative being borrowing from my parents and being strangled by the strings.

My mother is strangely quiet all the way to her house. She doesn't tell me what a loser Drew Scoones is—despite his good looks—and how I was obviously drooling over him. She doesn't ask me where Howard is taking me tonight or warn me not to tell my father about what happened because he will worry about us both and no doubt insist we see our respective psychiatrists.

She fidgets nervously, opening and closing her purse over and over again.

"You okay?" I ask her. After all, she's just found a dead man on the toilet, and tough as she is that's got to be upsetting.

When she doesn't answer me I pull over to the side of the road.

"Mom?" She refuses to meet my eyes. "You want me to take you to see Dr. Cohen?"

She looks out the window as if she's just realized we're on Broadway in Woodmere. "Aren't we near Marvin's Jewelers?" she asks, pulling something out of her purse.

"What have you got, Mother?" I ask, prying open her fingers to find the murdered man's ring.

"It was on the sink," she says in answer to my dropped jaw. "I was going to get his name and address and have you return it to him so that he could ask you out. I thought it was a sign that the two of you were meant to be together."

"He's dead, Mom. You understand that,

right?" I ask. You never can tell when my mother is fine and when she's in la-la land.

"Well, I didn't know that," she shouts at me. "Not at the time."

I ask why she didn't give it to Drew, realize that she wouldn't give Drew the time in a clock shop and add, "…or one of the other policemen?"

"For heaven's sake," she tells me. "The man is dead, Teddi, and I took his ring. How would that look?"

Before I can tell her it looks just the way it is, she pulls out a cigarette and threatens to light it.

"I mean, really," she says, shaking her head like it's my brains that are loose. "What does he need with it now?"